ACCLAIM FOR ALEX RIDER:

"Explosive, thrilling, action-packed – meet Alex Rider." **Guardian**

"Horowitz is pure class, stylish but action-packed ... being James Bond in miniature is way cooler than being a wizard." **Daily Mirror**

"Horowitz will grip you with suspense, daring and cheek – and that's just the first page! ... Prepare for action scenes as fast as a movie." **The Times**

"Anthony Horowitz is the lion of children's literature." **Michael Morpurgo**

"Fast and furious." **Telegraph**

"The perfect hero ... genuine 21st century stuff." **Daily Telegraph**

"Brings new meaning to the phrase 'action-packed'." **Sunday Times**

"Every bored schoolboy's fantasy, only a thousand times funnier, slicker and more exciting ... genius." **Independent on Sunday**

Titles by Anthony Horowitz

The Alex Rider series:
Stormbreaker
Point Blanc
Skeleton Key
Eagle Strike
Scorpia
Ark Angel
Snakehead
Crocodile Tears
Scorpia Rising
Russian Roulette

The Power of Five (Book One): *Raven's Gate*
The Power of Five (Book Two): *Evil Star*
The Power of Five (Book Three): *Nightrise*
The Power of Five (Book Four): *Necropolis*
The Power of Five (Book Five): *Oblivion*

The Devil and his Boy
Granny
Groosham Grange
Return to Groosham Grange
The Switch
More Bloody Horowitz

The Diamond Brothers books:
The Falcon's Malteser
Public Enemy Number Two
South by South East
The French Confection
The Greek Who Stole Christmas
The Blurred Man
I Know What You Did Last Wednesday

ALEX RIDER

ACTION
ADRENALINE
ADVENTURE

POINT BLANC

ANTHONY HOROWITZ

WALKER
BOOKS

For WS and N

First published 2001 by Walker Books Ltd
87 Vauxhall Walk, London SE11 5HJ

This edition published 2015

8 10 9 7

Text © 2001 Stormbreaker Productions Ltd
Cover illustration © 2015 Walker Books Ltd
Trademarks Alex Rider™; Boy with Torch Logo™
© 2010 Stormbreaker Productions Ltd

The right of Anthony Horowitz to be identified as author of this work has been asserted by him in accordance with the Copyright, Designs and Patents Act 1988

This book has been typeset in Officina Sans

Printed and bound in Great Britain by Clays Ltd, St Ives plc

British Library Cataloguing in Publication Data:
a catalogue record for this book
is available from the British Library

ISBN 978-1-4063-6020-2

www.walker.co.uk

CONTENTS

GOING DOWN

Michael J. Roscoe was a careful man.

The car that drove him to work at seven fifteen each morning was a custom-made Mercedes with reinforced-steel doors and bullet-proof windows. His driver, a retired FBI agent, carried a Beretta sub-compact semi-automatic pistol and knew how to use it. There were just five steps from the point where the car stopped to the entrance of Roscoe Tower on New York's Fifth Avenue, but CCTV cameras followed him every inch of the way. Once the automatic doors had slid shut behind him, a uniformed receptionist – also armed – watched as he crossed the foyer and entered his own private lift.

The lift had white marble walls, a blue carpet, a silver handrail and no buttons. Roscoe pressed his hand against a small glass panel. A sensor read his fingerprints, verified them and activated the lift. The doors slid shut and the lift rose to the sixtieth floor without stopping. Nobody else ever used it. Nor did it ever stop at any of the other floors in the building. While it was travelling up, the receptionist was on the telephone, letting Mr Roscoe's staff know that he was on his way.

Everyone who worked in Roscoe's private office had been hand-picked and thoroughly vetted. It was impossible to see him without an appointment. Getting an appointment could take three months.

When you're rich, you have to be careful. There are cranks, kidnappers, terrorists ... the desperate and the dispossessed. Michael J. Roscoe was the chairman of Roscoe Electronics and the ninth or tenth richest man in the world – and he was very careful indeed. Ever since his face had appeared on the front cover of *Time* magazine ("The Electronics King") he had realized that he had become a visible target. So when in public he walked quickly, with his head bent. The glasses that he wore had been chosen to hide as much as possible of his round, handsome face. His suits were expensive but anonymous. If he went to the theatre or to dinner, he always arrived at the last minute, preferring not to hang around. There were dozens of different security systems in his life and although they had once annoyed him, he had allowed them to become routine.

But ask any spy or security agent. Routine is the one thing that can get you killed. It tells the enemy where you're going and when you're going to be there. Routine was going to kill Michael J. Roscoe and this was the day death had chosen to come calling.

Of course, Roscoe had no idea of this as he stepped out of the lift directly into his private office – a huge room occupying the corner of the building, with floor-to-ceiling windows giving views in two directions; Fifth Avenue to the north, Central Park to the west. The two remaining walls contained a door, a low bookshelf and, next to the lift, a single oil painting: a vase of flowers by Vincent Van Gogh.

The black glass surface of his desk was equally uncluttered. A computer, a leather notebook, a telephone and a framed photograph of a fourteen-year-old boy. As he took off his jacket and sat down, Roscoe found himself looking at the picture of the boy. Blond hair, blue eyes and freckles. Paul Roscoe looked remarkably like his father forty years ago. Roscoe was now fifty-four, beginning to show his age despite his year-round tan. His son was almost as tall as him. The picture had been taken the summer before, on Long Island. They had spent the day sailing. Then they'd had a barbecue on the beach. It had been one of the few happy days they'd ever had together.

The door opened and his secretary came in. Helen Bosworth was English. She had left her home and her husband to come and work in New York and loved every minute of it. She had been working in this office for eleven years, and in all that time she had never forgotten a detail or made a mistake.

"Good morning, Mr Roscoe," she said.

"Good morning, Helen."

She set down a folder on his desk. "The latest figures from Singapore. Costings on the R-15 Organizer. You have lunch with Senator Andrews at twelve-thirty. I've booked the Ivy—"

"Did you remember to call London?" Roscoe asked.

Helen Bosworth blinked. She never forgot anything, so why had he asked? "I spoke to Alan Blunt's office yesterday afternoon," she said. Afternoon in New York would have been evening in London. "Mr Blunt was not available but I've arranged a person-to-person call for you this afternoon. We can have it patched through to your car."

"Thank you, Helen."

"Shall I have your coffee sent through to you?"

"No thank you, Helen. I won't have coffee today."

Helen Bosworth left the room, seriously alarmed. No coffee? Whatever next? Mr Roscoe had begun his day with a double espresso for as long as she had known him. Could it be that he was ill? He certainly hadn't been himself recently ... not since Paul had got back from that school in the South of France. And this phone call to Alan Blunt in London! Nobody had ever told her who he was but she had seen his name in a file once. He was something to do with British military intelligence. MI6. What was Mr Roscoe doing talking to a spy?

Helen Bosworth returned to her office and soothed her nerves, not with a coffee – she couldn't stand the stuff – but with a refreshing cup of English breakfast tea. Something very strange was going on and she didn't like it. She didn't like it at all.

*　　　*　　　*

Meanwhile, sixty floors below, a man had walked into reception wearing grey overalls with an ID badge attached to his chest. The badge identified him as Sam Green, maintenance engineer with X-Press Elevators Inc. He was carrying a briefcase in one hand and a large silver toolbox in the other. He set them both down in front of the reception desk.

Sam Green was not his real name. His hair – black and a little greasy – was fake, as were his glasses, moustache and uneven teeth. He looked fifty years old but was actually nearer thirty. Nobody knew his real name but in the business he was in, a name was the last thing he could afford. He was known as the Gentleman and he was one of the highest paid and most successful contract killers in the world. He had been given his nickname because he always sent flowers to the families of his victims.

The receptionist glanced at him.

"I'm here for the elevator," he said. He spoke with a Bronx accent even though he had never spent more than a week there in his life.

"What about it?" the receptionist asked. "You people were here last week."

"Yeah. Sure. We found a defective cable on elevator twelve. It had to be replaced but we didn't have the parts. So they sent me back." The Gentleman fished in his pocket and pulled out a crumpled sheet of paper. "You want to call Head Office? I've got my orders here."

If the receptionist had called X-Press Elevators Inc., he would have discovered that they did indeed employ a Sam Green – although he hadn't shown up for work for two days. This was because the real Sam Green was at the bottom of the Hudson River with a knife in his back and a twenty-pound block of concrete attached to his feet. But the receptionist didn't make the call. The Gentleman had guessed he wouldn't bother. After all, the lifts were always breaking down. There were engineers in and out the whole time. What difference would one more make?

The receptionist jerked a thumb. "Go ahead!" he said.

The Gentleman put away the letter, picked up his case and his toolbox, and went over to the lifts. There were a dozen public lifts servicing the skyscraper, plus a thirteenth for Michael J. Roscoe. Lift number twelve was at the end. As he went in, a delivery boy with a parcel tried to follow. "Sorry," the Gentleman said. "Closed for maintenance." The doors slid shut. He was on his own. He pressed the button for the sixty-first floor.

He had been given this job only a week before. He'd had to work fast – killing the real maintenance engineer, taking his identity, learning the layout of Roscoe Tower and getting his hands on the sophisticated piece of equipment he had known he would need. His employers wanted the multi-millionaire eliminated as quickly as possible. More importantly, it had to look like an accident. For this, the Gentleman had demanded – and been paid – two hundred thousand American dollars. The money was to be paid into a bank account in Switzerland; half now, half on completion.

The lift door opened. The sixty-first floor was used mainly for maintenance. This was where the water tanks were housed, also the computers that controlled the heat, air-conditioning, security cameras and lifts throughout the building. The Gentleman turned off the lift, using the manual override key that had once belonged to Sam Green, then went over to the computers. He knew exactly where they were. In fact, he could have found them wearing a blindfold. He opened his briefcase. There were two sections to the case. The lower part was a laptop computer. The lid was fitted out with a number of drills and other tools, each of them strapped into place.

It took him fifteen minutes to cut his way into

the Roscoe Tower mainframe and connect his laptop to the circuitry inside. Hacking his way past the Roscoe security systems took a little longer, but at last it was done. He tapped a command into his keyboard. On the floor below, Michael J. Roscoe's private lift did something it had never done before. It rose up one extra floor – to level sixty-one. The door, however, remained closed. The Gentleman did not need to get in.

Instead, he picked up the briefcase and the silver toolbox and carried them back into the same lift he had taken from reception. He turned the over-ride key and pressed the button for the fifty-ninth floor. Once again, he deactivated the lift. Then he reached up and pushed. In the top of the lift was a trapdoor that opened outwards. He pushed the briefcase and the silver box ahead of him, then pulled himself up and climbed onto the roof of the lift. He was now standing inside the main lift-shaft of Roscoe Tower. He was surrounded on four sides by girders and pipes blackened with oil and dirt. Thick steel cables hung down, some of them humming as they carried their loads up and down. Looking down, he could see a seemingly endless square tunnel, illuminated only by the chinks of light from the doors that slid open and shut again as the other lifts arrived at various floors. Somehow the breeze had made its way in from the street, spinning dust that stung his eyes. Next to him was a set of lift doors which, had he opened them, would have led him straight into Roscoe's office. Above these, over his head and a few metres to the right, was the underbelly of Roscoe's private lift.

The toolbox was next to him, on the lift roof. Carefully, he opened it. The sides of the case were lined with thick sponge. Inside, in the specially moulded space, was what looked like a complicated film projector, silver and concave with a thick glass lens. He took it out, then glanced at his watch. Eight thirty-five. It would take him an hour to connect the device to the bottom of Roscoe's lift, and a little more to ensure it was working. He had plenty of time.

Smiling to himself, the Gentleman took out a power screwdriver and began to work.

At twelve o'clock, Helen Bosworth called through on the telephone. "Your car is here, Mr Roscoe."

"Thank you, Helen."

Roscoe hadn't done much that morning. He had been aware that only half his mind was on his work. Once again, he glanced at the photograph on his desk. Paul. How could things have gone so wrong between a father and a son? And what could have happened in the last few months to make them so much worse?

He stood up, put his jacket on and walked across his office – on his way to lunch with Senator Andrews. He often had lunch with politicians. They either wanted his money, his ideas … or him. Anyone as rich as Roscoe was a powerful friend and politicians need all the friends they can get.

He pressed the lift call button and the doors slid open. He took one step forward.

The last thing Michael J. Roscoe saw in his life was a lift with white marble walls, a blue carpet and a silver handrail. His right foot, wearing one of the black leather shoes that were hand-made for him by a small shop in Rome, travelled down to the carpet and kept going … right through it. The rest of his body followed, tilting into the lift and then through it. And then he was falling sixty floors to his death. He was so surprised by what had happened, so totally unable to understand what had happened, that he didn't even cry out. He simply fell into the blackness of the lift-shaft, bounced twice off the walls, then crashed into the solid concrete of the basement, two hundred metres below.

The lift remained where it was. It looked solid but in fact it wasn't there at all. What Roscoe had stepped into was a hologram being projected into the empty space of the lift-shaft where the real lift should have been. The Gentleman had programed the door to open when Roscoe pressed the call button, and had quietly watched him step into oblivion. If the billionaire had just looked up for a moment, he would have seen the silver hologram projector beaming the image, a few metres above him. But a man getting into a lift on his way to lunch does not look up. The Gentleman had known this. And he was never wrong.

At twelve thirty-five, the chauffeur called up to say that Mr Roscoe hadn't arrived at the car. Ten minutes later, Helen Bosworth alerted security, who began to search the foyer of the building. At one o'clock, they called the restaurant. The senator was there, waiting for his lunch guest. But Roscoe hadn't shown up.

In fact, his body wasn't discovered until the next day, by which time the billionaire's disappearance had become the lead story on American TV news. A bizarre accident – that's what it looked like. Nobody could work out what had happened. Because of course, by that time, the Gentleman had reprogramed the mainframe, removed the projector and left everything as it should have been before quietly leaving the building.

Two days later, a man who looked nothing like a maintenance engineer walked into JFK International Airport. He was about to board a flight for Switzerland. But first of all he visited a flower shop and ordered a dozen black tulips to be sent to a certain address. The man paid with cash. He didn't leave a name.

BLUE SHADOW

The worst time to feel alone is when you're in a crowd. Alex Rider was walking across the playground, surrounded by hundreds of boys and girls of about his own age. They were all heading in the same direction, all wearing the same blue and grey uniform, all of them probably thinking much the same thoughts. The last lesson of the day had just ended. Homework, tea and television would fill the remaining hours until bed. Another school day. So why did he feel so out of it, as if he were watching the last weeks of the term from the other side of a giant glass screen?

Alex jerked his backpack over one shoulder and continued towards the bike shed. The bag was heavy. As usual, it contained double homework ... French and history. He had missed two weeks of school and he was having to work hard to catch up. His teachers had not been sympathetic. Nobody had said as much, but when he had finally returned with a doctor's letter (...*a bad dose of flu with complications*...) they had nodded and smiled and secretly thought him a little bit pampered and spoiled. On the other hand, they had to make allowances. They all knew that Alex had no parents, that he had been living with an uncle who had died in some sort of car accident. But even so. Two weeks in bed! Even his closest friends had to admit that was a bit much.

And he couldn't tell them the truth. He wasn't allowed to tell anyone what had really happened. That was the hell of it.

Alex looked around him, at the children streaming through the school gates, some dribbling footballs, some on their mobile phones. He looked at the teachers, curling themselves into their second-hand cars. At first, he had thought that the whole school had somehow changed while he was away. But he knew now that what had happened was worse. Everything was the same. It was he who had changed.

Alex was fourteen years old, an ordinary schoolboy in an ordinary west London comprehensive.

Or he had been. Only a few weeks ago, he had discovered that his uncle had been a secret agent, working for MI6. The uncle – Ian Rider – had been murdered and MI6 had forced Alex to take his place. They had given him a crash course in SAS survival techniques and sent him on a lunatic mission on the south coast. He had been chased, shot at and almost killed. And at the end of it he had been packed off and sent back to school as if nothing had happened. But first they had made him sign the Official Secrets Act. Alex smiled at the memory of it. He didn't need to sign anything. Who would have believed him anyway?

But it was the secrecy that was getting to him now. Whenever anyone asked him what he had been doing in the weeks he'd been away, he'd been forced to tell them that he'd been in bed, reading, slouching around the house, whatever. Alex didn't want to boast about what he'd done, but he hated having to deceive his friends. It made him angry. MI6 hadn't just put him in danger. They'd locked his whole life in a filing cabinet and thrown away the key.

He had reached the bike shed. Somebody muttered a "goodbye" in his direction and he nodded, then reached up to brush away the single strand of fair hair that had fallen over his eye.

Sometimes he wished that the whole business with MI6 had never happened. But at the same time – he had to admit it – part of him wanted it all to happen again. Sometimes he felt that he no longer belonged in the safe, comfortable world of Brookland School. Too much had changed. And at the end of the day, anything was better than double homework.

He lifted his bike out of the shed and unlocked it. Then he clipped on his helmet, pulled the backpack over his shoulders and prepared to ride away. That was when he saw the beat-up white car. Back again outside the school gates. For the second time that week.

Everyone knew about the man in the white car.

He was in his twenties, bald, and had two broken stumps where his front teeth should have been and five metal studs in his ear. He didn't advertise his name. When people talked about him, they called him Skoda – after the make of his car. But there were some who said that his name was Jake and he had once been at Brookland. If so, he had come back like an unwelcome ghost; here one minute, vanishing the next – somehow always a few seconds ahead of any passing police car or over-inquisitive teacher.

Skoda sold drugs. He sold soft drugs to the

younger kids and harder stuff to any of the sixth-formers stupid enough to buy it. It seemed incredible to Alex that Skoda could get away with it so easily, dealing his little packets in broad daylight. But of course there was a code of honour in the school. No one turned anyone into the police, not even a rat like Skoda. And there was always the fear that if Skoda went down, some of the people he supplied – friends, classmates – might go with him.

Drugs had never been a huge problem at Brookland, but recently that had begun to change. A clutch of seventeen-year-olds had started buying Skoda's goods and, like a stone dropped into a pool, the ripples had rapidly spread. There had been a spate of thefts, as well as one or two bullying incidents – younger children being forced to bring in money for older kids. The stuff Skoda was selling seemed to get more expensive the more you bought of it – and it hadn't been cheap at the start.

Alex watched as a heavy-shouldered boy with dark hair and serious acne lumbered over to the car, paused by the window and then continued on his way. He felt a sudden jolt of anger. The boy's name was Colin and just twelve months ago he had been one of Alex's best friends. In fact,

Colin had been popular with everyone. But then everything had changed. He had become moody and withdrawn. His work had gone downhill. Suddenly nobody had wanted to know him – and this was the reason. Alex had never thought much about drugs, apart from knowing that he would never take them himself. But he could see that the man in the white car wasn't just poisoning a handful of dumb kids. He was poisoning the whole school.

A policeman on foot patrol appeared, walking towards the gate. A moment later, the white car was gone, black smut bubbling from a faulty exhaust. Alex was on his bike before he knew what he was doing, pedalling fast out of the playground, swerving round the school secretary, who was also on her way home.

"Not too fast, Alex!" she called out, and sighed when he ignored her. Miss Bedfordshire had always had a soft spot for Alex without knowing quite why. And she alone in the school had wondered if there hadn't been more to his absence that the doctor's note had suggested.

The white Skoda accelerated down the road, turning left, then right, and Alex thought he was going to lose it. But then it twisted through the maze of back streets that led up to the King's Road and hit the inevitable four o'clock traffic jam, coming to a halt about two hundred metres ahead.

The average speed of traffic in London, even in the twenty-first century, is lower than it used to be in Victorian times. During normal working hours, any bicycle will beat any car on just about any journey at all. And Alex wasn't riding just any bike. He still had his Condor Junior Roadracer, hand-built for him in the workshop that had been open for business in the same street in Holborn for more than fifty years. He'd recently had it upgraded with an integrated brake and gear-lever system fitted to the handlebar, and he only had to flick his thumb to feel the bike click up a gear, the lightweight titanium sprockets spinning smoothly beneath him.

He caught up with the car just as it turned the corner and joined the rest of the traffic on the King's Road. He would just have to hope that Skoda was going to stay in the city, but some-how Alex didn't think it likely that he would travel too far. The drug dealer hadn't chosen Brook-land School as a target simply because he'd been there. It had to be somewhere in his general neighbourhood – not too close to home but not too far either.

The lights changed and the white car jerked

forward, heading west. Alex was pedalling slowly, keeping a few cars behind, just in case Skoda happened to glance in his mirror. They reached the corner known as World's End and suddenly the road was clear and Alex had to switch gears again and pedal hard to keep up. The car drove on, through Parson's Green and down towards Putney. Alex twisted from one lane to another, cutting in front of a taxi and receiving the blast of a horn as his reward. It was a warm day and he could feel his French and history homework dragging down his back. How much further were they going? And what would he do when they got there? Alex was beginning to wonder if this had been a good idea when the car turned off and he realized they had arrived.

Skoda had pulled into a rough tarmac area, a temporary carpark next to the River Thames, not far from Putney Bridge. Alex stayed on the bridge, allowing the traffic to roll past, and watched as the drug dealer got out of his car and began to walk. The area was being redeveloped, another block of prestige flats rising up to bruise the London skyline. Right now, the building was no more than an ugly skeleton of steel girders and prefabricated concrete slabs. It was surrounded by a swarm of men in hard hats. There were bulldozers, cement mixers and, towering above them all, a huge canary-yellow crane. A sign read:

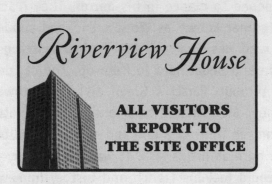

Riverview House

**ALL VISITORS
REPORT TO
THE SITE OFFICE**

Alex wondered if Skoda had some sort of business on the site. He seemed to be heading for the entrance. But then he turned off. Alex watched him, puzzled.

The building site was wedged in between the bridge and a cluster of modern buildings. There was a pub, then what looked like a brand-new conference centre, and finally a police station with a carpark half-filled with official cars. But right next to the building site, sticking out into the river, was a wooden jetty with two cabin cruisers and an old iron barge quietly rusting in the murky water. Alex hadn't noticed the jetty at first, but Skoda walked straight onto it, then climbed onto the barge. He opened a door and disappeared inside. Was this where he lived? It was late in the day. Somehow, Alex doubted he was about to set off on a pleasure cruise down the River Thames.

He got back on his bike and cycled slowly to the end of the bridge, and then down towards the carpark. He unclipped his helmet and left it with the backpack and the bike which he pushed out of sight then continued on foot, moving more slowly as he approached the jetty. He wasn't afraid of being caught. This was a public place and even if Skoda did reappear, there would be nothing he could do. But he was curious. Just what was the drug dealer doing onboard a barge? It seemed a bizarre place to have stopped. Alex still wasn't sure what he was going to do, but he wanted to have a look inside. Then he would decide.

The wooden jetty creaked under his feet as he stepped onto it. The barge was called *Blue Shadow* but there was little blue left in the flaking paint, the rusty ironwork and the dirty, oil-covered decks. The barge was about ten metres long and very square, with a single cabin in the centre. It was lying low in the water and Alex guessed that most of the living quarters would be underneath. He knelt down on the jetty and pretended to tie his shoelaces, hoping to look through the narrow, slanting windows. But all the curtains were drawn. What now?

The barge was moored on one side of the jetty. The two cruisers were side by side on the other. Skoda wanted privacy – but he must also need light, and there would be no need to draw the curtains on the far side with nothing there apart from the river. The only trouble was, to look in the other windows Alex would have to climb onto the barge itself. He considered briefly. It had to be worth the risk. He was near enough to the building site. Nobody was going to try to hurt him with so many people around.

He placed one foot on the deck, then slowly transferred his weight onto it. He was afraid that moving the barge would give him away. Sure enough, the barge dipped under his weight; but Alex had chosen his moment well. A police launch was sailing past, heading up the river and back into town. The barge bobbed naturally in its wake and by the time it settled Alex was onboard, crouching next to the cabin door.

Now he could hear music coming from inside. The heavy beat of a rock band. He didn't want to do it, but he knew there was only one way to look in. He tried to find an area of the deck that wasn't too covered in oil, then lay flat on his stomach. Clinging onto the handrail, he lowered his head and shoulders over the side of the barge and shifted himself forward so that he was hanging almost upside-down over the water.

He was right. The curtains on this side of the barge were open. Looking through the dirty glass of the window, he could see two men. Skoda was sitting on a bunk, smoking a cigarette. There was a second man, blond-haired and ugly, with twisted lips and three days' stubble, wearing a torn sweatshirt and jeans, making a cup of coffee at a small stove. The music was coming from an old-fashioned radio perched on a shelf. Alex looked around the cabin. Apart from two bunks and the miniature kitchen, the barge offered no living accommodation at all. Instead it had been converted for another purpose. Skoda and his friend had turned it into a floating laboratory.

There were two metal work-surfaces, a sink and a pair of electric scales. Everywhere there were test-tubes and Bunsen burners, flasks, glass pipes and measuring spoons. The whole place was filthy – obviously neither of the men cared about hygiene – but Alex knew that he was looking into the heart of their operation. This was where they prepared the drugs they sold; cut them down, weighed them and packaged them for delivery to local schools. It was an incredible idea – to put a drugs factory on a boat, almost in the middle of London and only a stone's throw away from a police station. But at the same time, it was a clever one. Who would have looked for it here?

The blond man suddenly turned round and Alex hooked his body up and slithered backwards onto the deck. For a moment he was dizzy. Hanging upside-down, the blood had drained into his head. He took a couple of breaths, trying to collect his thoughts. It would be easy enough to walk over to the police station and tell the officer in charge what he had seen. The police could take over from there.

But something inside Alex rejected the idea. Maybe that was what he would have done a few months before. Let someone else take care of it. But he hadn't cycled all this way just to call in the police. He thought back to his first sighting of the white car outside the school gates. He remembered Colin, his friend, shuffling over to it and felt once again a brief blaze of anger. This was something he wanted to do himself.

What could he do? If the barge had been equipped with a plug, Alex would have pulled it out and sunk the entire thing. But of course it wasn't as easy as that. The barge was tied to the jetty by two thick ropes. He could untie them

– but that wouldn't help either. The barge would drift away – but this was Putney; there were no whirlpools or waterfalls. Skoda would simply turn the engine on and cruise back again.

Alex looked around him. On the building site, the day's work was coming to an end. Some of the men were already leaving and, as he watched, he saw a trapdoor open about a hundred metres above him and a stocky man begin the long climb down from the top of the crane. Alex closed his eyes. A whole series of images had suddenly flashed into his mind, like different sections of a jigsaw.

The barge. The building site. The police station. The crane with its great hook dangling underneath the jib.

And Blackpool funfair. He'd gone there once with his housekeeper, Jack Starbright, and had watched as she'd won a teddy bear, hooking it out of a glass case with a mechanical claw and carrying it over to a chute.

Could it be done? Alex looked again, working out the angles. Yes. It probably could.

He stood up and crept back across the deck to the door that Skoda had entered. There was a length of wire lying to one side and he picked it up, then wound it several times round the handle of the door. He looped the wire over a hook in the wall and pulled it tight. The door was effectively locked. There was a second door at the back of the boat. Alex secured that one with his own bicycle padlock. As far as he could see, the windows were too narrow to crawl through. There was no other way in or out.

He crept off the barge and back onto the jetty. Then he untied it, leaving the thick rope loosely curled up beside the metal pegs – the stanchions – that had secured it. The river was still. It would be a while before the barge drifted away.

He straightened up. Satisfied with his work so far, he began to run.

HOOKED

The entrance to the building site was crowded with construction workers preparing to go home. Alex was reminded of Brookland an hour earlier. Nothing really changed when you got older – except that maybe you weren't given homework. The men and women drifting out of the site were tired, in a hurry to be away. That was probably why none of them tried to stop Alex as he slipped in among them, walking purposefully as if he knew where he was going, as if he had every right to be there.

But the shift wasn't completely finished yet. Other workers were still carrying tools, stowing away machinery, packing up for the night. They were all wearing protective headgear and, seeing a pile of plastic helmets, Alex snatched one up and put it on. The great sweep of the block of flats that was being built loomed up ahead of him. To pass through it he was forced into a narrow corridor between two scaffolding towers. Suddenly a thick-set man in white overalls stepped in front of him, blocking his way.

"Where are you going?" he demanded.

"My dad..." Alex gestured vaguely in the direction of another worker and kept walking. The trick worked. The man didn't challenge him again.

He was heading for the crane. It was standing in the open, the high priest of the construction. Alex hadn't realized how very tall it was until he reached it. The supporting tower was bolted into a massive block of concrete. The tower was very narrow – once he had squeezed through the iron girders he could reach out and touch all four sides. A ladder ran straight up the centre. Without stopping to think – if he thought about it he might change his mind – Alex began to climb.

It's only a ladder, he told himself. You've climbed ladders before. You've got nothing to worry about.

But this was a ladder with three hundred rungs. If Alex let go or slipped, there would be nothing to stop him falling to his death. There were rest platforms at intervals but Alex didn't dare stop to catch his breath. Somebody might look up and see him. And there was always a chance that the barge, loose from its moorings, might begin to drift.

After two hundred and fifty rungs, the tower narrowed. Alex could see the crane's control cabin directly above him. He looked back down. The men on the building site were suddenly very small and far away. He climbed the last stretch of ladder. There was a trapdoor over his head, leading into the cabin. But the trapdoor was locked.

Fortunately, Alex was ready for this. When MI6 had sent him on his first mission, they had given him a number of gadgets – he couldn't exactly call them weapons – to help him out of tight corners. One of these was a tube marked ZIT-CLEAN, FOR HEALTHIER SKIN. But the cream inside the tube did much more than clean up spots.

Although Alex had used most of it, he had managed to hold onto the last remnants and often carried the tube with him, as a sort of souvenir. He had it in his pocket now. Holding onto the ladder with one hand, he took the tube out with the other. There was very little of the cream left but Alex knew that a little was all he would need. He opened the tube, squeezed some of the cream onto the lock and waited. There was a moment's pause, then a hiss and a wisp of smoke. The cream was eating into the metal. The lock sprang open. Alex pushed back the trapdoor and climbed the last few rungs. He was in.

He had to close the trapdoor again to create enough floor space to stand on. He found himself in a square metal box, about the same size as a sit-in arcade game. There was a pilot's chair with two joysticks – one on each arm – and, instead of a screen, a floor-to-ceiling window with a spectacular view of the building site, the river and the whole of west London. A small computer monitor had been built into one corner and, at knee level, there was a radio transmitter.

The joysticks on the arms were surprisingly uncomplicated. Each had just six buttons. There were even helpful diagrams to show what they did. The right hand would lift the hook up and down. The left hand would move it along the jib – closer to or further from the cabin. The left hand also controlled the whole top of the crane, rotating it 360 degrees. It couldn't have been much simpler. Even the start button was clearly labelled. A big button for a big toy. Alex couldn't help smiling as he reached out for the controls. This was going to be like Christmas come early.

He pushed the button and felt power surge into the control cabin. The computer lit up with a graphic of a barking dog as the warm-up program came into life. Alex eased himself into the operator's chair. There were still twenty or thirty men on the site. Looking down between his knees, he could see them moving silently far below. Nobody had noticed that anything was wrong. But he knew he still had to move fast.

He pressed the green button on the right-hand control – green for go – then touched his fingers against the joystick and pushed. Nothing happened! Alex frowned. Maybe it was going to be more complicated than he'd thought. What had he missed? He rested his hands on the joysticks, looking left and right for another control. His right hand moved slightly and suddenly the hook soared up from the ground. It was working!

Unknown to Alex, when he gripped the handles of the joysticks, heat sensors concealed inside had read his body temperature and activated the crane. All modern cranes have the same security system built into them, in case the operator has a heart attack and falls against the controls. There can be no accidents. Body heat is needed to make the crane work.

Luckily for him, this crane was a Liebherr 154

EC-H, one of the most modern in the world. The Liebherr is incredibly easy to use – and remarkably accurate. Now Alex pushed sideways with his left hand and gasped as the crane swung round. In front of him he could see the jib stretching out, swinging high over the rooftops of London. The more he pushed, the faster the crane went. The movement couldn't have been smoother. The Liebherr 154 has a fluid coupling between the electric motor and the gears so that it never jolts or shudders – it glides. Alex found a white button under his thumb and pressed it. The movement stopped at once.

He was ready. He would need some beginner's luck, but he was sure he could do it – provided nobody looked up and saw the crane moving. He pushed with his left hand again and this time waited as the jib of the crane swung all the way round past Putney Bridge and over the River Thames. When the jib was pointing directly over the barge, he stopped. Now he manoeuvred the cradle with the hook. First he slid it right to the end of the jib. Then, using his other hand, he lowered it; quickly to begin with, more slowly as it drew closer to ground level. The hook was solid metal. If he hit the barge, Skoda might hear it and Alex would have given himself away. Carefully now, one centimetre at a time. Alex licked his lips and, using all his concentration, took careful aim.

The hook crashed into the deck. Alex cursed. Surely Skoda would have heard it and would even now be grappling with the door. Then he remembered the radio. Hopefully, the music would have drowned out the noise. He lifted the hook, at the same time dragging it across the deck towards him. He had seen his target. There was a thick metal stanchion welded into the deck at the near end. If he could just loop the hook around the stanchion he would have caught his fish. Then he could reel it in.

His first attempt missed the stanchion by more than a metre. Alex forced himself not to panic. He had to do this slowly or he would never do it at all. Working with his left and right hands, balancing one movement against the other, he dragged the hook over the deck and then back towards the stanchion. He would just have to hope that the radio was still playing and that the sliding metal wasn't making too much noise. He missed the stanchion a second time. This wasn't going to work!

No. He could do it. It was the same as the funfair ... just bigger. He gritted his teeth and manoeuvred the hook a third time. This time he saw it happen. The hook caught hold of the stanchion. He had it!

He looked down. Nobody had noticed anything wrong. Now ... how did you lift? He pulled with his right hand. The cable became taut. He actually felt the crane take the weight of the barge. The whole tower tilted forward alarmingly and Alex almost slid out of his seat. For the first time he wondered if his plan was actually possible. Could the crane lift the barge out of the water? What was the maximum load? There was a white placard at the end of the crane arm, printed with a measurement: 3900KG. Surely the boat couldn't weigh that much. He glanced at the computer screen. One set of digits was changing so rapidly he was unable to read them. They were showing the weight that the crane was taking. What would happen if the boat was too heavy? Would the computer initiate an automatic cut-out? Or would the whole thing just fall over?

Alex settled himself in the chair and pulled back, wondering what would happen next.

Inside the boat, Skoda was opening a bottle of gin. He'd had a good day, selling more than a hundred pounds' worth of merchandise to the kids at his old school. And the best thing was, they'd all be back for more. Soon he'd only sell them the stuff if they promised to introduce it to their friends. Then the friends would become customers too. It was the easiest market in the world. He'd got them hooked. They were his to do with as he liked.

The blond-haired man he was working with was called Mike Beckett. The two of them had met in prison and had decided to go into business together when they got out. The boat had been Beckett's idea. There was no proper kitchen, no toilet and it was freezing in winter ... but it worked. It even amused them to be so close to a police station. They enjoyed watching the police cars or boats – going past. Of course, the pigs would never think of looking right on their own doorstep.

Suddenly Beckett swore. "What the...?"

"What is it?" Skoda looked up.

"The cup..."

Skoda watched as a cup of coffee, which had been sitting on a shelf, began to move. It slid sideways, then fell off with a clatter, spilling cold coffee on the grey rag they called a carpet. Skoda was confused. The cup seemed to have moved on its own. Nothing had touched it. He giggled. "How did you do that?" he asked.

"I didn't."

"Then..."

Beckett was the first to realize what was happening – but even he couldn't guess the truth. "We're sinking!" he shouted.

He scrabbled for the door. Now Skoda felt it for himself. The floor was tilting. Test-tubes and beakers slid into each other then crashed to the floor, glass shattering. He swore and followed Beckett – uphill now. With every second that passed, the rake was becoming steeper. But the strange thing was that the barge didn't seem to be sinking at all. On the contrary, the front of it seemed to be rising out of the water.

"What's going on?" he yelled.

"The door's jammed!" Beckett had managed to open it a crack, but the padlock on the other side was holding it firm.

"There's the other door!"

But the second door was now high above them. Bottles rolled off the table and smashed. In the kitchen, soiled plates and mugs slid into each other, pieces flying. With something between a sob and a snarl, Skoda tried to climb up the mountainside that the inside of the boat had become. But it was already too steep. The door was almost over his head. He lost his balance and fell backwards, shouting as – one second later – the other man was thrown on top of him. The two of them rolled into the corner, tangled up in each other. Plates, cups, knives, forks and dozens of pieces of scientific equipment crashed into them. The walls of the barge were grinding with the pressure. A window shattered. A table turned itself into a battering-ram and hurled itself at them. Skoda felt a bone snap in his arm and screamed out loud.

The barge was completely vertical, hanging above the water at 90 degrees. For a moment it rested where it was. Then it began to rise...

Alex stared at the barge in amazement. The crane was lifting it at half speed – some sort of override had come into action, slowing the operation down – but it wasn't even straining. Alex could feel the power under his palms. Sitting in the cabin with both hands on the joysticks, his feet apart and the jib of the crane jutting out ahead of him, he felt as if he and the crane had become one. He only had to move a centimetre and the boat would be brought to him. He could see it, dangling on the hook, spinning slowly. Water was streaming off the stern. It was already clear of the water, rising up about a metre every five seconds. He wondered what it must be like inside.

The radio beside his knee hissed into life.

"Crane operator! This is base. What the hell do you think you're doing? Over!" A pause, a burst of static. Then the metallic voice was back. "Who is in the crane? Who's up there? Identify yourself!"

There was a microphone snaking towards Alex's chin and he was tempted to say something. But he decided against it. Hearing a teenager's voice would only panic them more.

He looked down. There were about a dozen construction workers closing in on the base of the crane. Others were pointing at the boat, jabbering amongst themselves. No sounds reached the cabin. It was as if Alex was cut off from the real world. He felt very secure. He had no doubt that more workers would have already started climbing the ladder and that it would all be over soon, but for the moment he was untouchable. He concentrated on what he was doing. Getting the barge out of the water had been only half his plan. He still had to finish it.

"Crane operator! Lower the hook! We believe there are people inside the boat and you are endangering their lives. Repeat. Lower the hook!"

The barge was high above the water, dangling on the end of the hook. Alex moved his left hand, turning the crane round so that the boat was swung in an arc along the river and then over dry land. There was a sudden buzz. The jib came to a halt. Alex pushed the joystick. Nothing happened. He glanced at the computer. The screen had gone blank.

Someone at ground level had come to their senses and done the only sensible thing. They had switched off the power. The crane was dead.

Alex sat where he was, watching the barge swaying in the breeze. He hadn't quite succeeded in what he had set out to do. He had planned to lower the boat – along with its contents – safely into the carpark of the police station. It would have made a nice surprise for the authorities, he had thought. Instead, the boat was now hanging over the conference centre that he had seen from Putney Bridge. But at the end of the day, he didn't suppose it made much difference. The end result would be the same.

He stretched his arms and relaxed, waiting for the trapdoor to burst open. This wasn't going to be easy to explain.

And then he heard the tearing sound.

The metal stanchion that protruded from the end of the deck had not been designed to carry the entire weight of the barge. It was a miracle that it had lasted as long as it had. As Alex watched, open-mouthed, from the cabin, the stanchion tore itself free. For a few seconds it clung by one edge to the deck. Then the last metal rivet came loose.

The barge had been sixty metres above the ground. Now it began to fall.

In the Putney Riverside Conference Centre, the chief constable of the Metropolitan Police was addressing a large crowd of journalists, TV cameras, civil servants and government officials. He was a tall, thin man who took himself very seriously. His dark blue uniform was immaculate, every piece of silver – from the studs on his epaulettes to his five medals – was polished until it gleamed. This was his big day. He was sharing the platform with no less a personage than the home secretary himself. The assistant chief constable was there and also seven lower-ranking officers. A slogan was being projected onto the wall behind him.

WINNING THE WAR
AGAINST DRUGS

Silver letters on a blue background. The chief

constable had chosen the colours himself, knowing that they matched his uniform. He liked the slogan. He knew that it would be in all the major newspapers the next day – and, just as important, a photograph of himself.

"We have overlooked nothing!" he was saying, his voice echoing around the modern room. He could see the journalists scribbling down his every word. The television cameras were all focused on him. "Thanks to my personal involvement and efforts, we have never been more successful. Home Secretary..." He smiled at the senior politician, who smiled toothily back. "But we are not resting on our laurels. Oh no! Any day now we hope to announce another breakthrough."

That was when the barge hit the glass roof of the conference centre. There was an explosion. The chief constable just had time to dive for cover as a vast, dripping object plunged down towards him. The home secretary was thrown backwards, his spectacles flying off his face. His security men froze, helpless. The boat crashed into the space in front of them, between the stage and the audience. The side of the cabin had been torn off and what was left of the laboratory was exposed, with the two dealers sprawled together in one corner, staring dazedly at the hundreds of policemen and officials who now surrounded them. A cloud of white powder mushroomed up and then fell onto the dark blue uniform of the chief constable, covering him from head to toe. The fire alarms had gone off. The lights fused and went out. Then the screaming began.

Meanwhile, the first of the construction workers had made it to the crane cabin and was gazing in astonishment at the fourteen-year-old boy he had found there.

"Do you...?" he stammered. "Do you have any idea what you've just done?"

Alex glanced at the empty hook and at the gaping hole in the roof of the conference centre, at the rising smoke and dust. He shrugged apologetically.

"I was just working on the crime figures," he said. "And I think there's been a drop."

SEARCH AND REPORT

At least they didn't have far to take him.

Two men brought Alex down from the crane, one above him on the ladder and one below. The police were waiting at the bottom. Watched by the incredulous construction workers, he was frog-marched off the building site and into the police station just a few buildings away. As he passed the conference centre, he saw the crowds pouring out. Ambulances had already arrived. The home secretary was being whisked away in a black limousine. For the first time, Alex was seriously worried, wondering if anyone had been killed. He hadn't meant it to end like this.

Once they got to the police station, everything happened in a whirl of slamming doors, blank official faces, whitewashed walls, forms and phone calls. Alex was asked his name, his age, his address. He saw a police sergeant tapping the details into a computer: but what happened next took him by surprise. The sergeant pressed ENTER and visibly froze. He turned and looked at Alex, then hastily left his seat. When Alex had entered the police station he'd been the centre of attention, but suddenly everyone was avoiding his eye. A more senior officer appeared. Words were exchanged. Alex was led down a corridor and put into a cell.

Half an hour later, a female police officer appeared with a tray of food. "Supper," she said.

"What's happening?" Alex asked. The woman smiled nervously, but said nothing. "I left my bike by the bridge," Alex said.

"It's all right, we've got it." She couldn't leave the room fast enough.

Alex ate the food: sausages, toast, a slice of cake. There was a bunk in the room and, behind a screen, a sink and a toilet. He wondered if anyone was going to come in and talk to him, but nobody did. Eventually he fell asleep.

The next thing he knew, it was seven o'clock in the morning. The door was open and a man he knew only too well was standing in the cell, looking down at him.

"Good morning, Alex," he said.

"Mr Crawley."

John Crawley looked like a junior bank manager and when Alex had first met him he had indeed been pretending that he worked for a bank. The cheap suit and striped tie could both have come from a Marks & Spencer "Boring Businessman" range. In fact, Crawley worked for MI6. Alex wondered if the clothes were a cover or a personal choice.

"You can come with me now," Crawley said. "We're leaving."

"Are you taking me home?" Alex asked. He wondered if anyone had been told where he was.

"No. Not yet."

Alex followed Crawley out of the building. This time there were no police officers in sight. A car with a driver stood waiting outside. Crawley got into the back with Alex.

"Where are we going?" Alex asked.

"You'll see." Crawley opened a copy of the *Daily Telegraph* and began to read. He didn't speak again.

They drove east through the city and up towards Liverpool Street. Alex knew at once where he was being taken and, sure enough, the car turned into the entrance of a seventeen-storey building near the station and disappeared down a ramp into an underground carpark. Alex had been here before. The building pretended to be the head-quarters of the Royal & General bank. In fact, this was where the Special Operations division of MI6 was based.

The car stopped. Crawley folded his paper away and got out, ushering Alex ahead of him. There was a lift in the basement and the two of them took it to the sixteenth floor.

"This way." Crawley gestured to a door marked 1605. The Gunpowder Plot, Alex thought. It was an absurd thing to flash into his mind, a frag-ment of the history homework he should have been doing the night before. 1605 – the year Guy Fawkes had tried to blow up the Houses of Parliament. Oh well, it looked as if the homework was going to have to wait.

Alex opened the door and went in. Crawley didn't follow. When Alex looked round, he was already walking away.

"Shut the door, Alex, and come in."

Once again, Alex found himself standing opposite the prim, unsmiling man who headed the Special Operations division of MI6. Grey suit, grey face, grey life ... Alan Blunt seemed to belong to an entirely colourless world. He was sitting behind a wooden desk in a large, square office that could have belonged to any business anywhere in the world. There was nothing personal in the room, not even a picture on the wall or a photograph on the desk. Even the pigeons pecking on the window-sill outside were grey.

Blunt was not alone. Mrs Jones, his senior officer, was with him, sitting on a leather chair, wearing a mud-brown jacket and dress, and – as usual – sucking a peppermint. She looked up at Alex with black, bead-like eyes. She seemed to be more pleased to see him than her boss was. It was she who had spoken. Blunt had barely registered the fact that Alex had come into the room.

Then Blunt looked up. "I hadn't expected to see you again so soon," he said.

"That's just what I was going to say," Alex replied. There was a single empty chair in the office. He sat down.

Blunt slid a sheet of paper across his desk and examined it briefly. "What on earth were you thinking of?" he demanded. "This business with the crane? You've done an enormous amount of damage. You've practically destroyed a two million pound conference centre. It's a miracle nobody was killed."

"The two men in the boat will be in hospital for

months," Mrs Jones added.

"You could have killed the home secretary!" Blunt continued. "That would have been the last straw. What *were* you doing?"

"They were drug dealers," Alex said.

"So we've discovered. But the normal procedure would have been to dial 999."

"I couldn't find a phone." Alex sighed. "They turned off the crane," he explained. "I was going to put the boat in the carpark."

Blunt blinked once and waved a hand as if dismissing everything that had happened. "It's just as well that your special status came up on the police computer," he said. "They called us – and we've handled the rest."

"I didn't know I had special status," Alex said.

"Oh yes, Alex. You're nothing if not special." Blunt gazed at him for a moment. "That's why you're here."

"So you're not going to send me home?"

"No. The fact is, Alex, we were thinking of contacting you anyway. We need you again."

"You're probably the only person who can do what we have in mind," Mrs Jones added.

"Wait a minute!" Alex shook his head. "I'm far enough behind at school as it is. Suppose I'm not interested?"

Mrs Jones sighed. "We could of course return you to the police," she said. "As I understand it, they were very keen to interview you."

"And how is Miss Starbright?" Blunt asked.

Jack Starbright – the name was short for Jackie or Jacqueline, Alex wasn't sure which – was the housekeeper who had been looking after Alex since his uncle had died. She was a bright, red-haired American girl who had come to London to study law but had never left. Blunt wasn't interested in her health, Alex knew that. The last time they'd met, he'd made his position clear. So long as Alex did as he was told, he could stay living in his uncle's house with Jack. Step out of line and she'd be deported to America and Alex would be taken into care. It was blackmail of course, pure and simple.

"She's fine," Alex said. There was quiet anger in his voice.

Mrs Jones took over. "Come on, Alex," she said. "Why pretend you're an ordinary schoolboy any more?"

She was trying to sound more friendly, more like a mother. But even snakes have mothers, Alex thought.

"You've already proved yourself once," she went on. "We're just giving you a chance to do it again."

"It'll probably come to nothing," Blunt continued. "It's just something that needs looking into. What we call a search and report."

"Why can't Crawley do it?"

"We need a boy."

Alex fell silent. He looked from Blunt to Mrs Jones and back again. He knew that neither of them would hesitate for a second before pulling him out of Brookland and sending him to the grimmest institution they could find. And anyway, wasn't this what he had been asking for only the day before? Another adventure. Another chance to save the world.

"All right," he said. "What is it this time?"

Blunt nodded at Mrs Jones, who unwrapped a sweet and began.

"I wonder if you know anything about a man called Michael J. Roscoe?" she asked.

Alex thought for a moment. "He was that businessman who had an accident in New York." He'd seen the news on TV. "Didn't he fall down a liftshaft or something?"

"Roscoe Electronics is one of the largest companies in America," Mrs Jones said. "In fact it's one of the largest in the world. Computers, printers, laptops ... everything from mobile phones to washing-machines. Roscoe was very rich, very influential—"

"And very short-sighted," Alex cut in.

"It certainly seems to have been a very strange and even a careless accident," Mrs Jones agreed. "The lift somehow malfunctioned. Roscoe didn't look where he was going. He fell into the lift-shaft and died. That's the general opinion. However, we're not so sure."

"Why not?"

"First of all, there are a number of details that don't add up. On the day Roscoe died, a maintenance engineer by the name of Sam Green called at Roscoe Tower on Fifth Avenue. We know it was Green – or someone who looked very much like him – because we've seen him. They have CCTV cameras and he was filmed going in. He said he'd come to look at a defective cable. But according to the company that employed him, there was no defective cable and he certainly wasn't acting under orders from them."

"Why don't you talk to him?"

"We'd like to. But Green has vanished without trace. We think he might have been killed. We think someone might have taken his place and somehow set up the accident that killed Roscoe."

Alex shrugged. "I'm sorry. I'm sorry about Mr Roscoe. But what's it got to do with me?"

"I'm coming to that." Mrs Jones paused. "The strangest thing of all is that, the day before he died, Roscoe telephoned this office. A personal call. He asked to speak to Mr Blunt."

"I met Roscoe at Cambridge University," Blunt said. "That was a long time ago. We became friends."

That surprised Alex. He didn't think of Blunt as the sort of man who had friends. "What did he say?" he asked.

"Unfortunately, I wasn't here to take the call," Blunt replied. "I arranged to speak with him the following day. By that time, it was too late."

"Do you have any idea what he wanted?"

"I spoke to his assistant," Mrs Jones said. "She wasn't able to tell me very much, but she understood that Roscoe was concerned about his son. He has a fourteen-year-old son, Paul Roscoe."

A fourteen-year-old son. Alex was beginning to see the way things were going.

"Paul was his only son," Blunt explained. "I'm afraid the two of them had a very difficult relationship. Roscoe divorced a few years ago and although the boy chose to live with his father, they didn't really get on. There were the usual teenage problems, but of course, when you grow up surrounded by millions of dollars these problems sometimes get amplified. Paul was doing badly at school. He was playing truant, spending time with some very undesirable friends. There was an incident with the New York police – nothing serious and Roscoe managed to hush it up, but it still upset him. I spoke to Roscoe from time to time. He was worried about Paul and felt the boy was out of control. But there didn't seem to be very much he could do."

"So is that what you want me for?" Alex interrupted. "You want me to meet this boy and talk to him about his father's death?"

"No." Blunt shook his head and handed a file to Mrs Jones.

She opened it. Alex caught a glimpse of a photograph; a dark-skinned man in military uniform. "Remember what we told you about Roscoe," she said. "Because now I want to tell you about another man." She slid the photograph round so that Alex could see it. "This is General Viktor Ivanov. Ex-KGB. Until last December he was head of the Foreign Intelligence Service and probably the second or third most powerful man in Russia after the president. But then something happened to him too. It was a boating accident on the Black Sea. His cruiser exploded ... nobody knows why."

"Was he a friend of Roscoe's?" Alex asked.

"They probably never met. But we have a department here that constantly monitors world news, and their computers have thrown up a very strange coincidence. Ivanov also had a fourteen-year-old son, Dimitry. And one thing is certain. The young Ivanov certainly knew the young Roscoe because they went to the same school."

"Paul and Dimitry..." Alex was puzzled. "What was a Russian boy doing at a school in New York?"

"He wasn't in New York." Blunt took over. "As I told you, Roscoe was having trouble with his boy. Trouble at school, trouble at home. So last year he decided to take action. He sent Paul to Europe, to a place in France, a sort of finishing school. Do you know what a finishing school is?"

"I thought it was the sort of place where rich people used to send their daughters," Alex said. "To learn table manners."

"That's the general idea. But this school is for boys only, and not just ordinary boys. The fees are twenty thousand pounds a term. This is the brochure. You can have a look." He passed a heavy, square booklet to Alex. Written on the cover, gold letters on black, were the two words:

POINT BLANC

"It's right on the French-Swiss border," Blunt explained. "South of Geneva. Just above Grenoble, in the French Alps. It's pronounced *Point Blanc*." He spoke the words with a French accent. "Literally, *white point*. It's a remarkable place. Built as a private home by some lunatic in the nineteenth century. As a matter of fact, that's what it became after he died ... a lunatic asylum. It was taken over by the Germans in the Second World War. They used it as a leisure centre for their senior staff. After that, it fell into disrepair until it was bought by the current owner, a man called Grief. Dr Hugo Grief. He's the principal of the school. What I suppose you'd call the head-teacher."

Alex opened the brochure and found himself looking at a colour photograph of Point Blanc. Blunt was right. The school was like nothing he had ever seen; something between a German castle and a French chateau, straight out of a Grimm's fairy tale. But what drew Alex's breath, more than the building itself, was the setting. The school was perched on the side of a mountain, with nothing but mountains all around; a great pile of brick and stone surrounded by a snow-covered landscape. It seemed to have no business being there, as if it had been snatched out of an ancient city and accidentally dropped there. No roads led to the school. The snow continued all the way to the front gate. But looking again, Alex saw a modern helicopter pad projecting over the battlements. He guessed that was the only way to get there ... and to leave.

He turned the page.

Welcome to the Academy at
POINT BLANC...

the introduction began. It had been printed in the sort of lettering Alex would expect to find on the menu of an expensive restaurant.

...a unique school that is much more than a school, created for boys who need more than the ordinary education system can provide. In our time we have been called a school for "problem boys", but we do not believe the term applies.

There are problems and there are boys. It is our aim to separate the two.

"There's no need to read all that stuff," Blunt said. "All you need to know is that the academy takes in boys who have been expelled from all their other schools. There are never very many of them there. Just six or seven at a time. And it's unique in other ways too. For a start, it only takes the sons of the super-rich—"

"At twenty thousand pounds a term, I'm not surprised," Alex said.

"You'd be surprised just how many parents have applied to send their sons there," Blunt went on. "But I suppose you've only got to look at the newspapers to see how easy it is to go off the rails when you're born with a silver spoon in your mouth. It doesn't matter if they're politicians or popstars; fame and fortune for the parents often brings problems for the children ... and the more successful the parents are, the more pressure there seems to be. The academy went into business to sort the young people out, and by all accounts it's been a great success."

"It was established twenty years ago," Mrs Jones said. "In that time it's had a client list you'd find hard to believe. Of course, they've kept the names confidential. But I can tell you that parents who have sent their children there include an American vice-president, a Nobel

Prize-winning scientist and a member of our own royal family!"

"As well as Roscoe and this man, Ivanov," Alex said.

"Yes."

Alex shrugged. "So it's a coincidence. Just like you said. Two rich parents with two rich kids at the same school. They're both killed in accidents. Why are you so interested?"

"Because I don't like coincidence," Blunt replied. "In fact, I don't believe in coincidence. Where some people see coincidence, I see conspiracy. That's my job."

And you're welcome to it, Alex thought. He said, "Do you really think the school and this man Grief might have had something to do with the two deaths? Why? Had they forgotten to pay the fees?"

Blunt didn't smile. "Roscoe telephones me because he's worried about his son. The next day he's dead. We've also learned from Russian intelligence sources that a week before he died, Ivanov had a violent argument with his son. Apparently Ivanov was worried about something. Now do you see the link?"

Alex thought for a moment. "So you want me to go to this school," he said. "How are you going to manage that? I don't have parents and they were never rich anyway."

"We've already arranged that," Mrs Jones said. Alex realized that she must have made her plans before the business with the crane ever happened. Even if he hadn't drawn attention to himself, they would have come for him. "We're going to supply you with a wealthy father. His name is Sir David Friend."

"Friend ... as in Friend's supermarkets?" Alex had seen the name often enough in the newspapers.

"Supermarkets. Department stores. Art galleries. Football teams." Mrs Jones paused. "Friend is certainly a member of the same club as Roscoe. The billionaires' club. He's also heavily involved in government circles, as personal adviser to the prime minister. Very little happens in this country without Sir David being involved in some way."

"We've created a false identity for you," Blunt said. "From this moment on, I want you to start thinking of yourself as Alex Friend, the fourteen-year-old son of Sir David."

"It won't work," Alex said. "People must know that Friend doesn't have a son."

"Not at all." Blunt shook his head. "He's a very

private person and we've created the sort of son no father would want to talk about. Expelled from Eton. A criminal record ... shoplifting, vandalism and possession of drugs. That's you, Alex. Sir David and his wife, Caroline, don't know what to do with you. So they've enrolled you in the academy. And you've been accepted."

"And Sir David has agreed to all this?" Alex asked.

Blunt sniffed. "As a matter of fact, he wasn't very happy about it – about using someone as young as you. But I spoke to him at some length and, yes, he agreed to help."

"So when am I going to the academy?"

"Five days from now," Mrs Jones said. "But first you have to immerse yourself in your new life. When you leave here, we've arranged for you to be taken to Sir David's home. He has a house in Lancashire. He lives there with his wife – and he has a daughter. She's one year older than you. You'll spend the rest of the week with the family, which should give you time to learn everything you need to know. It's vital that you have a strong cover. After that, you'll leave for Grenoble."

"And what do I do when I get there?"

"We'll give you a full briefing nearer the time.

Essentially, your job is to find out everything you can. It may be that this school is perfectly ordinary and that there was in fact no connection between the deaths. If so, we'll pull you out. But we want to be sure."

"How will I get in touch with you?"

"We'll arrange all that." Mrs Jones ran an eye over Alex, then turned to Blunt. "We'll have to do something about his appearance," she said. "He doesn't exactly look the part."

"See to it," Blunt said.

Alex sighed. It was strange really. He was simply going from one school to another. From a London comprehensive to a finishing school in France. It wasn't quite the adventure he'd been expecting.

He stood up and followed Mrs Jones out of the room. As he left, Blunt was already sifting through documents as if he'd forgotten that Alex had been there or even existed at all.

THE SHOOTING PARTY

The chauffeur-driven Rolls-Royce Corniche cruised along a tree-lined avenue, penetrating ever deeper into the Lancashire countryside, its 6.75 litre light pressure V8 engine barely a whisper in the great green silence all around. Alex sat in the back, trying to be unimpressed by a car that cost as much as a house. Forget the Wilton wool carpets, the wooden panelling and the leather seats, he told himself. It's only a car.

It was the day after his meeting at MI6 and, as Mrs Jones had promised, his appearance had completely changed. He had to look like a rebel – the rich son who wanted to live life by his own rules. So Alex had been dressed in purposefully provocative clothes. He was wearing a hooded sweatshirt, skinny jeans – frayed at the ankles – and Nike limited edition trainers that were falling apart on his feet. Despite his protests, his hair had been cut so short that he almost looked like a skinhead and his right ear had been pierced. He could still feel it throbbing underneath the temporary stud that had been put in to stop the hole closing.

The car had reached a set of wrought-iron gates which opened automatically to receive it. And there was Haverstock Hall, a great mansion with stone figures on the terrace and seven figures in the price. Sir David had bought it a few years ago, Mrs Jones had told him, because he wanted a place in the country. Half the Lancashire country-side seemed to have come with it. The grounds stretched for miles in every direction, with sheep dotted across the hills on one side and three horses watching from an enclosure on the other. The house itself was Georgian: white brick with slender windows and columns. Everything looked very neat. There was a walled garden with evenly spaced beds, a square glass conservatory hous-ing a swimming pool, and a series of ornamental hedges with every leaf perfectly in place.

The car stopped. The horses swung their necks round to watch Alex get out, their tails rhythmic-ally beating at flies. Nothing else moved.

The chauffeur walked round to the boot. "Sir

David will be inside," he said. He had disapproved of Alex from the moment he had set eyes on him. Of course, he hadn't said as much, he was too professional. But he showed it with his eyes.

Alex moved away from the car, drawn towards the conservatory on the other side of the drive. It was a warm day, the sun beating down on the glass, and the water on the other side looked suddenly inviting. He passed through a set of doors. It was hot inside the conservatory. The smell of chlorine rose up from the water, stifling him.

He had thought the pool was empty, but as he watched, a figure swam up from the bottom, breaking through the surface just in front of him. It was a girl, dressed in a white bikini. She had long black hair and dark eyes but her skin was pale. Alex guessed she must be about fifteen years old and remembered what Mrs Jones had told him about Sir David Friend. "He has a daughter ... one year older than you." So this must be her. He watched her pull herself out of the water. Her body was well-shaped, closer to the woman she would become than the girl she had been. She was going to be beautiful. That much was certain. The trouble was, she already knew it. When she looked at Alex, arrogance flashed in her eyes.

"Who are you?" she asked. "What are you doing in here?"

"I'm Alex."

"Oh yes." She reached for a towel and wrapped it around her neck. "Daddy said you were coming – but I didn't expect you to just walk in like this." Her voice was very adult and upper-class. It sounded strange, coming out of that fifteen-year-old mouth. "Do you swim?" she asked.

"Yes," Alex said.

"That's a shame. I don't like having to share the pool. Especially with a boy. And a smelly London boy at that." She ran her eyes over Alex, taking in the torn jeans, the shaven hair, the stud in his ear. She shuddered. "I can't think *what* Daddy was doing, agreeing to let you stay," she went on. "And having to pretend you're my brother! What a ghastly idea! If I did have a brother, I can assure you he wouldn't look like you."

Alex was wondering whether to pick the girl up and throw her back into the pool – or out through a window – when there was a movement behind him and he turned to see a tall, rather aristocratic man with curling grey hair and glasses, wearing a sports jacket, an open-necked shirt and cords. He too seemed a little jolted by Alex's appearance, but he recovered quickly, extending a hand. "Alex?" he enquired.

"Yes."

"I'm David Friend."

Alex shook his hand. "How do you do," he said politely.

"I hope you had a good journey. I see you've met my daughter." He smiled at the girl who was now sitting beside the pool drying herself, ignoring them both.

"We haven't actually introduced ourselves," Alex said.

"Her name is Fiona. I'm sure the two of you will get on fine." Sir David didn't sound convinced. He gestured back towards the house. "Why don't we go and talk in my study?"

Alex followed him back across the drive and into the house. The front door opened into a hall that could have come straight out of the pages of an expensive magazine. Everything was perfect, the antique furniture, ornaments and paintings placed exactly so. There wasn't a speck of dust to be seen and even the sunlight streaming in through the windows seemed almost artificial, as if it was only there to bring out the best in everything it touched. It was the house of a man who knows exactly what he wants and has the time and the money to get it.

"Nice place," Alex said.

"Thank you. Please come this way." Sir David opened a heavy, oak-panelled door to reveal a sophisticated, modern office beyond. There was a desk with a chair on either side, two computer screens, a white leather sofa and a series of metal bookshelves. Sir David showed Alex to a chair and sat down behind the desk.

He was unsure of himself. Alex could see it immediately. Sir David Friend might run a business empire worth millions – even billions – of pounds, but this was a new experience for him. Having Alex there, knowing who and what he was. He wasn't quite sure how to react.

"I've been told very little about you," he began. "Alan Blunt got in touch with me and asked me to put you up here for the rest of the week, to pretend that you're my son. I have to say, you don't look anything like me."

"I don't look anything like myself either," Alex said.

"You're on your way to some school in the French Alps. They want you to investigate it." He paused. "Nobody asked me my opinion," he said, "but I'll give it to you anyway. I don't like the idea of a fourteen-year-old boy being used as a spy. It's dangerous—"

"I can look after myself," Alex cut in.

"I mean, it's dangerous to the government. If you manage to get yourself killed and anyone finds out, it could cause the prime minister a great deal of embarrassment. I advised him against it, but for once he disagreed with me. It seems that the decision had already been made. This school – the academy – has already telephoned me to say that the assistant director will be coming here to pick you up next Saturday. It's a woman. A Mrs Stellenbosch. That's a South African name, I think…"

Sir David had a number of bulky files on his desk. He pushed them forward. "In the meantime, I understand you have to familiarize yourself with details about my family. I've prepared a number of files. You'll also find information here about the school you're meant to have been expelled from, Eton. You can start reading them tonight. If you need to know anything more, just ask. Fiona will be with you the whole time." He glanced down at his fingertips. "I'm sure that in itself will be quite an experience for you."

The door opened and a woman came in. She was slim and dark-haired, very much like her daughter. She was wearing a simple mauve dress with a string of pearls around her neck. "David..." she began, then stopped, seeing Alex.

"This is my wife," Friend said. "Caroline, this is the boy I was telling you about, Alex."

"It's very nice to meet you, Alex." Lady Caroline tried to smile but her lips only managed a faint twitch. "I understand you're going to stay with us for a while."

"Yes Mother," Alex said.

Lady Caroline blushed.

"He has to pretend to be our son," Sir David reminded her. He turned to Alex. "Fiona doesn't know anything about MI6 and the rest of it. I don't want to alarm her. I've told her that it's connected with my work ... a social experiment, if you like. She's to pretend you're her brother. To give you a week in the country as part of the family. I'd prefer it if you didn't tell her the truth."

"Dinner is in half an hour," Lady Caroline said. "Do you eat venison?" She sniffed. "Perhaps you'd like a wash before you eat? I'll show you to your room."

Sir David passed the files to Alex. "You've got a lot of reading to do. I'm afraid I have to go back to London tomorrow – I have lunch with the president of France – so I won't be able to help you. But, as I say, if there's anything you don't know—"

"Fiona Friend," Alex said.

Alex had been given a small, comfortable room at the back of the house. He took a quick shower, then put his old clothes back on again. He liked to feel clean, but he had to look grimy. It suited the character of the boy he was supposed to be. He opened the first of the files. Sir David had been thorough. He had given Alex the names and recent histories of just about the entire family, as well as photographs of holidays, details of the house in Mayfair, the flats in New York, Paris and Rome and the villa in Barbados. There were newspaper clippings, magazine articles ... everything he could possibly need.

A gong sounded. It was seven o'clock. Alex went downstairs and into the dining room. This was a room with six windows and a polished table long enough to seat sixteen. But there were only the three of them there: Sir David, Lady Caroline and Fiona. The food had already been served, presumably by a butler or maid. Sir David gestured to an empty chair. Alex sat down.

"Fiona was just talking about Don Giovanni," Lady Caroline said. There was a pause. "It's an opera. By Mozart."

"I'm sure Alex isn't interested in opera," Fiona said. She was in a bad mood. "In fact, I doubt if we have *anything* in common. Why do I have to pretend he's my brother? The whole thing is completely—"

"Fiona," Sir David muttered in a low voice.

"Well, it's all very well having him here, Daddy, but it *is* meant to be my Easter holiday." Alex realized that Fiona must go to a private school. Her term would have ended earlier than his. "I don't think it's fair."

"Alex is here because of my work," Sir David continued. It was strange, Alex thought, the way they talked about him as if he wasn't actually there. "I know you have a lot of questions, Fiona, but you're just going to have to do as I say. He's only with us until the end of the week. I want you to look after him."

"Is it something to do with the supermarkets?" Fiona asked.

"Fiona!" Sir David didn't want any more argument. "It's what I told you. An experiment. And you will make him feel welcome!"

Fiona picked up her glass and looked directly at Alex for the first time since he had come into the room. "We'll see about that," she said.

*　　*　　*

The week seemed endless. After only two days, Alex had decided that if he had really been a son in this frigid, self-important family, he probably *would* have ended up rebelling. Sir David had left at six o'clock the first morning and was still in London, sending emails to his wife and daughter. Lady Caroline did her best to avoid Alex. Once or twice she drove into the town nearby, but otherwise she seemed to spend a lot of time in bed. And Fiona...

When she wasn't quoting opera, she was boasting about her lifestyle, her wealth, her holidays around the world. At the same time, she made it clear how much she disliked Alex. She'd asked him several times what he was really doing at Haverstock Hall. Alex had shrugged and said nothing – which had made her dislike him all the more.

On the third day, she introduced him to some of her friends.

"I'm going shooting," she told him. "I don't suppose you want to come."

Alex shrugged. He had memorized most of the details in the files and figured he could easily pass as a member of the family. Now he was counting the hours until the woman from the academy arrived to take him away.

"Have you ever been shooting?" Fiona asked.

"No," Alex said.

"I go hunting and shooting," Fiona said. "But of course, you're a city boy. You wouldn't understand."

"What's so great about killing animals?" Alex asked.

"It's part of the country way of life. It's traditional." Fiona looked at him as if he were stupid. It was how she always looked at him. "Anyway, the animals enjoy it."

The shooting party turned out to be young and – apart from Fiona – entirely male. There were five of them waiting on the edge of a wood that was part of the Haverstock estate. Rufus, the leader, was sixteen, well-built with dark curly hair. He seemed to be Fiona's official boyfriend. The others – Henry, Max, Bartholomew and Fred – were about the same age. Alex looked at them with a heavy heart. They had uniform Barbour jackets, tweed trousers, flat caps and Huntsman leather boots. They spoke with uniform public school accents. Each of them carried a shotgun, with the barrel broken over his arm. Two of them were smoking. They gazed at Alex with barely concealed contempt. Fiona must have already told them about him. The London boy.

Quickly, she made the introductions. Rufus stepped forward.

"Nice to have you with us," he drawled. He ran his eyes over Alex. "Up for a bit of shooting are we?"

"I don't have a gun," Alex said.

"Well, I'm afraid I'm not going to lend you mine." Rufus snapped the barrel back into place and held it up for Alex to see. It was eighty centimetres of gleaming steel stretching out of a dark walnut stock decorated with ornately carved, solid silver sideplates. "It's an over-under shotgun with detachable trigger, hand-made by Abbiatico and Salvinelli," he said. "It cost me thirty grand – or my mother, anyway. It was a birthday present."

"It can't have been easy to wrap," Alex said. "Where did she put the ribbon?"

Rufus's smile faded. "You wouldn't know anything about guns," he said. He nodded at one of the other teenagers, who handed Alex a much more ordinary weapon. It was old and a little rusty. "You can use this one," he said. "And if you're very good and don't get in the way, maybe we'll let you have a cartridge."

They all laughed at that. Then the two smokers put out their cigarettes and they set off into the wood.

Thirty minutes later, Alex knew he had made a mistake in coming. The boys blasted away left and right, aiming at anything that moved. A rabbit spun in a glistening red ball. A wood pigeon tumbled out of the branches and flapped around on the leaves below. Whatever the quality of their weapons, the teenagers weren't good shots. Many of the animals they shot were only wounded, and Alex felt a growing sickness following this trail of blood.

They reached a clearing and paused to reload. Alex turned to Fiona. "I'm going back to the house," he said.

"Why? Can't stand the sight of a little blood?"

Alex glanced at a rabbit about fifty metres away. It was lying on its side with its back legs kicking helplessly. "I'm surprised they let you carry guns," he said. "I thought you had to be seventeen."

Rufus had overheard him. He stepped forward, an ugly look in his eyes. "We don't bother with rules in the countryside," he muttered.

"Maybe Alex is going to report us to the police!" Fiona said.

"The nearest police station is forty miles from here."

"You can call them ... if you can get a signal."

They all laughed again. Alex had had enough. Without saying another word, he turned round and walked off.

It had taken them thirty minutes to reach the clearing, but thirty minutes later he was still stuck in the wood, completely surrounded by trees and wild shrubs. Alex realized he was lost. He was annoyed with himself. He should have watched where he was going when he was following Fiona and the others. The wood was enormous. Walk in the wrong direction and he might blunder onto the moors ... and it could be days before he was found. At the same time, the spring foliage was so thick that he could barely see ten metres in any direction. How could he possibly find his way? And should he try to retrace his steps or continue forward in the hope of stumbling on the right path?

Alex sensed danger before the first shot was fired. Perhaps it was the snapping of a twig or the click of a metal bolt being slipped into place. He froze – and that was what saved him. There was an explosion – loud, close – and a tree one step ahead of him shattered, splinters of wood dancing in the air.

Alex turned round, searching for whoever had

fired the shot. "What are you doing?" he shouted. "You nearly hit me!"

Almost immediately there was a second shot and, just behind it, a whoop of excited laughter. And then Alex realized. They hadn't mistaken him for an animal. They were aiming at him for fun!

He dived forward and began to run. The trunks of the trees seemed to press in on him from all sides, threatening to bar his way. The ground beneath him was soft from recent rain and dragged at his feet, trying to glue them into place. There was a third explosion. He ducked, feeling the gunshot spray above his head, shredding the foliage.

Anywhere else in the world, this would have been madness. But this was the middle of the English countryside and these were rich, bored teenagers who were used to having things their own way. Alex had insulted them. Perhaps it had been the jibe about the wrapping paper. Perhaps it was his refusal to tell Fiona who he really was. But they had decided to teach him a lesson and they would worry about the consequences later. Did they mean to kill him? "We don't bother with rules in the countryside," Rufus had said. If Alex was badly wounded – or even killed – they would somehow get away with it. A dreadful accident.

He wasn't looking where he was going and stepped into the line of fire.

No. That was impossible.

They were trying to scare him, that was all.

Two more shots. A pheasant erupted out of the ground, a ball of spinning feathers, and screamed up into the sky. Alex ran on, his breath rasping in his throat. A thick briar reached out across his chest and tore at his clothes. He still had the gun he had been given and he used it to beat a way through. A tangle of roots almost sent him sprawling.

"Alex? Where *are* you?" The voice belonged to Rufus. It was high-pitched and mocking, coming from the other side of a barrier of leaves. There was another shot, but this one went high over his head. They couldn't see him. Had he got away?

Alex came to a stumbling, sweating halt. He had broken out of the wood but he was still hopelessly lost. Worse – he was trapped. He had come to the edge of a wide, filthy lake. The water was a scummy brown and looked almost solid. No ducks or wild birds were anywhere near the surface. The evening sun beat down on it and the smell of decay drifted up.

"He went that way!"

"No ... through here!"

"Let's try the lake..."

Alex heard the voices and knew that he couldn't let them find him here. He had a sudden image of his body, weighed down with stones, at the bottom of the lake. But that gave him an idea. He had to hide.

He stepped into the water. He would need something to breathe through. He had seen people do this in films. They would lie in the water and breathe through a hollow reed. But there were no reeds here. Apart from grass and thick, slimy algae, nothing was growing at all.

One minute later, Rufus appeared at the edge of the lake, his gun hooked over his arm. He stopped and looked around with eyes that knew the forest well. Nothing moved.

"He must have doubled back," he said.

The other hunters had gathered behind him. There was a tension between them now, a guilty silence. They knew the game had gone too far.

"Let's forget him," one of them said.

"Yeah."

"We've taught him a lesson."

They were in a hurry to get home. The group disappeared back the way they had come. Rufus was left on his own, still clutching his gun, searching for Alex. He took one last look across the water, then turned to follow them.

That was when Alex struck. He had been lying under the water, watching the vague shapes of the teenagers as if through a sheet of thick brown glass. The barrel of the shotgun was in his mouth. The rest of the gun was just above the surface of the lake. He was using the hollow tubes to breathe through. Now he rose up – a nightmare creature oozing mud and water, with fury in his eyes. Rufus heard him, but he was too late. Alex swung the shotgun, catching Rufus in the small of the back. Rufus grunted and fell to his knees, his own gun falling out of his hands. Alex picked it up. There were two cartridges in the breach. He snapped the gun shut.

Rufus looked at him and suddenly all the arrogance had gone and he was just a stupid, frightened teenager, struggling to get to his knees.

"Alex!" The single word came out as a whimper. It was as if he was seeing Alex for the first time. "I'm sorry!" he snivelled. "We weren't really going to hurt you. It was a joke. Fiona put us up to it. We just wanted to scare you. Please!"

Alex paused, breathing heavily. "How do I get out of here?" he asked.

"Just follow the lake round," Rufus said.

"There's a path..."

Rufus was still on his knees. There were tears in his eyes. Alex realized that he was pointing the silver-plated shotgun in his direction. He turned it away, disgusted with himself. This boy wasn't the enemy. He was nothing.

"Don't follow me," Alex said, and began to walk.

"Please...!" Rufus called after him. "Can I have my gun back? My mother would kill me if I lost it."

Alex stopped. He weighed the weapon in his hands, then threw it with all his strength. The hand-crafted Italian shotgun spun twice in the dying light then disappeared with a splash into the middle of the lake. "You're too young to play with guns," he said.

He walked away, letting the forest swallow him up.

THE TUNNEL

The man sitting in the gold, antique chair turned his head slowly and gazed out of the window at the snow-covered slopes of Point Blanc. Dr Hugo Grief was almost sixty years old with short white hair and a face that was almost colourless too. His skin was white, his lips vague shadows. Even his tongue was no more than grey. And yet, against this blank background, he wore circular wire spectacles with dark red lenses. The effect was startling. And, for him, the entire world would be the colour of blood. He had long fingers, the nails beautifully manicured. He was dressed in a dark suit buttoned up to his neck. If there were such a thing as a vampire, it would look very much like Hugo Grief.

"I have decided to move the Gemini Project

into its last phase," he said. He spoke with a South African accent, biting into each word before it left his mouth. "There can be no further delay."

"I understand, Dr Grief."

There was a woman sitting opposite Dr Grief, dressed in tight-fitting Lycra with a sweat band round her head. This was Eva Stellenbosch. She had just finished her morning work-out – two hours of weightlifting and aerobic exercise – and she was still breathing heavily, her huge muscles rising and falling. Mrs Stellenbosch had a facial structure that wasn't quite human, with lips curving out far in front of her nose and wisps of bright ginger hair hanging over a high-domed forehead. She was holding a glass filled with some milky green liquid. Her fingers were thick and stubby. She had to be careful not to break the glass.

She sipped her drink, then frowned. "Are you sure we're ready?" she asked.

"We have no choice in the matter. We have had two unsatisfactory results in the last few months. First Ivanov. Then Roscoe in New York. Quite apart from the expense of arranging the terminations, it's possible that someone may have connected the two deaths."

"Possible, but unlikely," Mrs Stellenbosch said.

"The intelligence services are idle and inefficient, it is true. The CIA in America. MI6 in England. Even the Russians! They're all shadows of what they used to be. But even so, there's always the chance that one of them might have accidentally stumbled onto something. The sooner we end this phase of the operation, the more chance we have of remaining ... unnoticed." Dr Grief brought his hands together and rested his chin on his fingertips. "When is the final boy arriving?" he asked.

"Alex?" Mrs Stellenbosch emptied her glass and set it down. She opened her handbag and took out a handkerchief which she used to wipe her lips. "I am travelling to England tomorrow," she said.

"Excellent. You'll take the boy to Paris on the way here?"

"Of course, Doctor. If that is what you wish."

"It is very much what I wish, Mrs Stellenbosch. We can do all the preliminary work there. It will save time. What about the Sprintz boy?"

"I'm afraid we still need another few days."

"That means that he and Alex will be here at the same time."

"Yes."

Dr Grief considered. He had to balance the risk

of the two boys meeting against the dangers of moving too fast. It was fortunate that he had a scientific mind. His calculations were never wrong. "Very well," he said. "The Sprintz boy can stay with us for another few days."

Mrs Stellenbosch nodded.

"Alex Friend is an excellent catch for us," Dr Grief said

"Supermarkets?" The woman sounded unconvinced.

"His father has the prime minister's ear. He is an impressive man. His son, I am sure, will meet all our expectations." Dr Grief smiled. His eyes glowed red. "Very soon, we'll have Alex here at the academy. And then, at last, the Gemini Project will be complete."

"You're sitting all wrong," Fiona said. "Your back isn't straight. Your hands should be lower. And your feet are pointing the wrong way."

"What does it matter, so long as you're enjoying yourself?" Alex asked, speaking through gritted teeth.

It was the fourth day of his stay at Haverstock Hall and Fiona had taken him out riding. Alex wasn't enjoying himself at all. Before the ride, he'd had to endure the inevitable lecture –

although he had barely listened. The horses were Iberian or Hungarian. They'd won a bucketful of gold medals. Alex didn't care. All he knew was that his horse was big and black and attracted flies. And that he was riding it with all the style of a sack of potatoes on a trampoline.

The two of them had barely mentioned the business in the forest. When Alex had limped back to the house, soaked and freezing, Fiona had politely fetched him a towel and offered him a cup of tea.

"You tried to kill me!" Alex said.

"Don't be silly!" Fiona looked at Alex with something like pity in her eyes. "We would never do that. Rufus is a very nice boy."

"What...?"

"It was just a game, Alex. Just a bit of fun."

And that was it. Fiona had smiled as if everything had been explained and then gone to have a swim. Alex had spent the rest of the evening with the files. He was trying to take in a fake history that lasted fourteen years. There were uncles and aunts, friends at Eton, a whole crowd of people he had to know without ever having met any of them. More than that, he was trying to get the feel of this luxurious lifestyle. That was why he was here now, out riding with Fiona –

she upright in her riding jacket and breeches, he bumping along behind.

They had ridden for about an hour and a half when they came to the tunnel. Fiona had tried to teach Alex a bit of technique – the difference, for example, between walking, trotting and cantering. But this was one sport he had already decided he would never take up. Every bone in his body had been rattled out of place and his bottom was so bruised he wondered if he would ever be able to sit down again. Fiona was enjoying his torment. He even wondered if she had chosen a particularly bumpy route to add to his bruises. Or maybe it was just a particularly bumpy horse.

There was a single railway line ahead of them, with an automatic level-crossing equipped with a bell and flashing lights to warn motorists of any approaching train. Fiona steered her horse – a smaller grey – towards it. Alex's horse automatically followed. He assumed they were going to cross the line, but when she reached the barrier, Fiona stopped.

"There's a short-cut we can take if you want to get home," she said.

"A short-cut would be great," Alex admitted.

"It's that way." Fiona pointed up the line, and

there was the tunnel, a gaping black hole in the side of a hill, surrounded by dark red Victorian brick. Alex looked at her to see if she was joking. She was obviously quite serious. He turned back to the tunnel. It was like the barrel of a gun, pointing at him, warning him to keep away. He could almost imagine the giant finger on the trigger, somewhere behind the hill. How long was it? Looking more carefully, he could see a pin-prick of light at the other end. Perhaps up to a kilometre away.

"You're not being serious," he said.

"Actually, Alex, I don't usually tell jokes. When I say something, I mean it. I'm just like my father."

"Your father isn't barking mad," Alex muttered.

Fiona pretended not to hear him. "The tunnel is exactly one kilometre long," she explained. "There's a bridge on the other side, then another level-crossing. If we go that way, we can be home in thirty minutes. Otherwise it's an hour and a half back the way we came."

"Then let's go the way we came."

"Oh Alex, don't be such a scaredy-cat!" Fiona pouted at him. "There's only one train an hour on this line and the next one isn't due for" – she looked at her watch – "twenty minutes. I've been through the tunnel a hundred times and it never takes more than five minutes. Less if you canter."

"It's still crazy to ride on a railway line."

"Well, you'll have to find your own way home if you turn back." She kicked with her heels and her horse jerked forward, past the barrier and onto the line. "I'll see you later."

But Alex followed her. He would never have been able to ride back to the house on his own. He didn't know the way and he could barely control the horse. Even now it was following Fiona with no prompting from him. Would the two animals really enter the darkness of the tunnel? It seemed incredible, but Fiona had said they'd done it before and sure enough the horse walked into the side of the hill without even hesitating.

Alex shivered as the light was suddenly cut off behind him. It was cold and clammy inside. The air smelled of soot and diesel. The tunnel was a natural echo-chamber. The horses' hooves rattled all around them as they struck against the gravel between the sleepers. What if his horse stumbled? Alex put the thought out of his mind. The leather saddles creaked. Slowly his eyes got used to the dark. A certain amount of sunshine was filtering in from behind. More comfortingly, the way out was visible straight ahead, the circle of light widening with every step as they drew nearer. He tried to relax. Perhaps this wasn't going to be so bad after all.

And then Fiona spoke. She had slowed down, allowing his horse to catch up with hers. "Are you still worried about the train, Alex?" she said. "Perhaps you'd like to go faster..."

He heard the riding crop whistle through the air and felt his horse jerk as Fiona whipped it hard on the rear. The horse whinnied and leapt forward. Alex was thrown backwards, almost off the saddle. Digging in with his legs he just managed to cling on, but the top half of his body was at a crazy angle, the reins tearing into the horse's mouth. Fiona laughed. Alex was aware only of the wind rushing past him, the thick blackness spinning round his face and the horse's hooves striking heavily at the gravel as the animal careered forward. Dust blew into his eyes, blinding him. He thought he was going to fall.

But then, miraculously, they had burst out into the light. Alex fought for his balance and brought the horse back under control, pulling back with the reins and squeezing the horse's flanks with his knees. He took a deep breath, spat out an oath and waited for Fiona to appear.

His horse had come to rest on the bridge that

she had mentioned. The bridge was fashioned out of thick iron girders and spanned a river. There had been a lot of rain that month and, about fifteen metres below him, the water was racing past, dark green and deep. Carefully, he turned round to face the tunnel. If he lost control here it would be easy to fall over the edge. The sides of the bridge couldn't have been more than a metre high.

He could hear Fiona approaching. She had been cantering after him, probably laughing the entire way. He gazed into the tunnel – and that was when the grey burst out, raced past him and disappeared through the level-crossing on the other side of the bridge.

But Fiona wasn't on it.

The horse had come out alone.

It took Alex a few seconds to work it out. His head was reeling. She must have fallen off. Perhaps her horse had stumbled. She could be lying inside the tunnel. On the track. How long was there until the next train? Twenty minutes, she had said. But at least five of those minutes had gone, and she might have been exaggerating to begin with. What should he do? He had only three choices.

Go back in on foot.

Go back in on the horse.

Go home and forget about her.

No. He had only two choices. He knew that. He swore for a second time, then seized hold of the reins. Somehow he would get this horse to obey him. He had to get the girl out and he had to do it fast.

Perhaps his desperation managed to communicate itself to the horse's brain. The animal wheeled round and tried to back away, but when Alex kicked with his heels it stumbled forward and reluctantly entered the darkness of the tunnel for a second time. Alex kicked again. He didn't want to hurt it but he could think of no other way to make it obey him.

The horse trotted on. Alex searched ahead. "Fiona!" he called out. There was no reply. He had hoped that she would be walking towards him, but he couldn't hear any footsteps. If only there was more light!

The horse stopped and there she was, right in front of him, lying on the ground, her arms and chest actually on the line. If a train came now, it would cut her in half. It was too dark to see her face, but when she spoke he heard the pain in her voice.

"Alex," she said. "I think I've broken my ankle."

"What happened?"

"There was a cobweb or something. I was trying to keep up with you. It went in my face and I lost my balance."

She'd been trying to keep up with him! She sounded as if she was blaming *him* – as if she'd forgotten that she had whipped his horse on in the first place.

"Can you get up?" Alex asked.

"I don't think so."

Alex sighed. Keeping a tight hold on the reins, he slid off his horse. Fiona couldn't have timed it better. She had fallen right in the middle of the tunnel. He forced himself not to panic. According to her calculations, the next train must still be at least ten minutes away. He reached down to help her up. His foot came to rest on one of the rails ... and he felt something. Under his foot. Shivering up his leg. The track was vibrating.

The train was on its way.

"You've got to stand up," he said, trying to keep the fear out of his voice. He could already see the train in his imagination, thundering along the line. When it plunged into the tunnel, it would be a five hundred tonne torpedo that would smash them to pieces. He could hear the grinding of the wheels, the roar of the engine.

Blood and darkness. It would be a horrible way to die.

But he still had time. "Can you move your toes?" he asked.

"I think so." Fiona was clutching onto him.

"Then your ankle's probably sprained, not broken. Come on."

He dragged her up, wondering if it would be possible to stay inside the tunnel, at the edge of the track. If they hugged the wall, the train might simply go past them. But Alex knew there wouldn't be enough space. And even if the train missed them, it would still hit the horse. Suppose it derailed? Dozens of people could be killed.

"What train comes this way?" he asked. "Does it carry passengers?"

"Yes." Fiona was sounding tearful. "It's a Virgin train. Heading up to Glasgow."

Alex sighed. It was just his luck to get a Virgin train that arrived on time.

Fiona froze. "What's that?" she asked.

She had heard the clanging of a bell. What was it? Of course – the level-crossing! It was signalling the approach of the train, the barrier lowering itself over the road.

And then Alex heard a second sound that made his blood run cold. For a moment he couldn't breathe. It was extraordinary. His breath had got stuck in his lungs and refused to get up to his mouth. His whole body was paralysed as if some switch had been thrown in his brain. He was simply terrified.

The screech of a train whistle. It was still a mile or more away but the tunnel was acting as a sound conductor and he could feel it almost cutting into him. And now there was another noise. The rolling thunder of the diesel engine. It was moving fast towards them. Underneath his foot, the rail was vibrating more violently.

Alex gulped for air and forced his legs to obey him. "Get on the horse," he shouted. "I'll help you."

Not caring how much pain he caused her, he dragged Fiona next to the horse and forced her up towards the saddle. The noise was getting louder with every second that passed. The rail was humming softly, like a giant tuning-fork. The very air inside the tunnel seemed to be in motion, spinning left and right as if trying to get out of the way.

Fiona squealed and Alex felt her weight leave his arms as she fell onto the saddle. The horse whinnied and took a half step sideways, and for a dreadful moment Alex thought she was going to ride off without him. There was just enough light to make out the shapes of both the animal and its rider. He saw Fiona grabbing the reins. She brought the horse back under control. Alex reached up and caught hold of its mane, using the thick hair to pull himself onto the saddle in front of Fiona. The noise of the approaching train was getting louder and louder. Soot and loose cement were trickling out of the curving walls. The wind currents were twisting faster, the rails singing. For a moment the two of them were tangled together, but then he had the reins and she was clinging onto him, her arms around his chest.

"Go!" he shouted, and kicked the horse.

The horse needed no encouragement. It raced for the light, galloping up the railway line, throwing Alex and Fiona back and forth into each other.

Alex didn't dare look behind him, but he felt the train as it reached the mouth of the tunnel and plunged into it, travelling at one hundred and five miles per hour. A shock wave hammered into them. The train was punching the air out of its way, filling the space with solid steel. The horse understood the danger and burst forward with new speed, its hooves flying over the sleepers in great strides. Ahead of them the tunnel mouth opened up but Alex knew, with a sickening sense of despair, that they weren't going to make it. Even when they got out of the tunnel, they would still be hemmed in by the sides of the bridge. The second level-crossing was a hundred metres further down the line. They might get out, but they would die in the open air.

The horse passed through the end of the tunnel. Alex felt the circle of darkness slip over his shoulders. Fiona was screaming, her arms wrapped around him so tightly that he could barely breathe. He could hardly hear her. The roar of the train was right behind him. As the horse began a desperate race over the bridge, he sneaked a glance round. He just had time to see the huge metallic beast roar out of the tunnel, towering over them, its body painted the brilliant red of the Virgin colours, the driver staring in horror from behind his window. There was a second blast from the train whistle, this one all-consuming, exploding all around them. Alex knew what he had to do. He pulled on one rein, kicking with the opposite foot at the same time. He just hoped the horse would understand what he wanted.

And somehow it worked. The horse veered round. Now it was facing the side of the bridge. There was a final, deafening blast from the train. Diesel fumes smothered them.

The horse jumped.

The train roared past, barely missing them. But now they were in the air, over the side of the bridge. The carriages were still thundering past; a red blur. Fiona screamed again. Everything seemed to be happening in slow motion as they fell. One moment they were next to the bridge, a moment later underneath it and still falling. The green river rose up to receive them.

The horse with its two riders plummeted through the air and crashed into the river. Alex just had time to snatch a breath. He was afraid the water wouldn't be deep enough, that all three of them would end up with broken bones. But then they had hit the surface and passed through, down into a freezing, dark green whirlpool that sucked at them greedily, threatening to keep them there for ever. Fiona was torn away from him. He felt the horse kick itself free. Bubbles exploded out of his mouth and he realized he was yelling.

Finally, Alex rose to the surface again. The water was rushing past and, dragged back by his clothes and shoes, he clumsily swam for the nearest bank.

The train driver hadn't stopped. Perhaps he

had been too frightened by what had happened. Perhaps he wanted to pretend it hadn't happened at all. The train had gone.

Alex reached the bank and pulled himself, shivering, onto the grass. There was a splutter and a cough from behind him and Fiona appeared. She had lost her riding hat and her long black hair was hanging over her face. Alex looked past her. The horse had also managed to reach dry land. It trotted forward and shook itself, seemingly unharmed. Alex was glad about that. At the end of the day, the horse had saved both their lives.

He stood up. Water dripped out of his clothes. There was no feeling anywhere in his body. He wondered if it was because of the cold water or the shock of what he had just been through. He went over to Fiona and helped her to her feet.

"Are you all right?" he asked.

"Yes." She was looking at him strangely. She wobbled and he put out a hand to steady her. "Thank you," she said.

"That's all right."

"No." She held onto his hand. Her shirt had fallen open and she threw back her head, shaking the hair out of her eyes. "What you did back there ... it was fantastic. Alex, I'm sorry I've been such a beast to you all week. I thought – because you were only here for charity and all the rest of it – I thought you were just an oik. But I was wrong about you. You're really great. And I know we're going to be friends now." She half closed her eyes and moved towards him, her lips slightly parted. "You can kiss me if you like," she said.

Alex let go of her and turned away. "Thanks, Fiona," he said. "But frankly I'd prefer to kiss the horse."

SPECIAL EDITION

The helicopter circled twice over Haverstock Hall before beginning its descent. It was a Robinson R44 four-seater aircraft, American-built. There was only one person – the pilot – inside. Sir David Friend had returned from London and he and his wife came outside to watch it land in front of the house. The engine noise died down and the rotors began to slow. The cabin door slid open and the pilot got out, dressed in a one-piece leather flying suit, helmet and goggles.

The pilot walked up to them, extending a hand. "Good morning," she said. "I'm Mrs Stellenbosch from the academy."

If Sir David and Lady Caroline had been thrown by their first sight of Alex, the appearance of this assistant director, as she called herself, left them frozen to the spot. Sir David was the first to recover. "You flew the helicopter yourself?"

"Yes, I'm qualified." Mrs Stellenbosch had to shout over the noise of the rotors, which were still turning.

"Would you like to come in?" Lady Caroline asked. "Perhaps you'd like some tea?"

She led them into the house and through to the living room, where Mrs Stellenbosch sat, her legs apart, her helmet on the sofa beside her. Sir David and Lady Caroline sat opposite her. Tea was brought in on a tray.

"Do you mind if I smoke?" Mrs Stellenbosch asked. She reached into a pocket and took out a small packet of cigars without waiting for an answer. She lit one and blew smoke. "What a very beautiful house you have, Sir David. Georgian, I would say, but decorated with such taste! And where, may I ask, is Alex?"

"He went for a walk," Sir David said.

"Perhaps he's a little nervous." She smiled again and took the teacup Lady Caroline had proffered. "I understand that Alex has been a great source of concern to you."

Sir David Friend nodded. His eyes gave nothing away. For the next few minutes, he told Mrs Stellenbosch about Alex, how he had been expelled from Eton, how out of control he had become. Lady Caroline listened to all this in silence, occasionally holding her husband's arm.

"I'm at my wit's end," Sir David concluded. "We have an older daughter and she's perfect. But Alex? He hangs around the house. He doesn't read. He doesn't show any interest in anything. His appearance ... well, you'll see for yourself. Point Blanc Academy is our last resort, Mrs Stellenbosch. We're desperately hoping you can sort him out."

The assistant director poked at the air with her cigar, leaving a grey trail. "I'm sure you've been a marvellous father, Sir David," she purred. "But these modern children! It's heart-breaking the way some of them behave. You've done the right thing in coming to us. As I'm sure you know, the academy has had a remarkable success rate over the past eleven years."

"What exactly do you do?" Lady Caroline asked.

"We have our methods." The woman's eyes twinkled. She tapped ash into her saucer. "But I can promise you, we'll sort out all Alex's problems. Don't you worry! When he comes home, he'll be a completely different boy!"

Meanwhile, Alex was crossing a field about a

kilometre away from the house. He had seen the helicopter land and knew that his time had come. But he wasn't ready to leave yet. Mrs Jones had telephoned him the night before. Once again, MI6 weren't going to send him into what might be enemy territory empty-handed.

He watched as a combine harvester rumbled slowly towards him, cutting a swathe through the grass. It jerked to a halt a short distance away and the door of the cabin opened. A man got out – with difficulty. He was so fat that he had to squeeze himself out, first one buttock, then the next, finally his stomach, shoulders and head. The man was wearing a checked shirt and blue overalls – a farmer's outfit. But even if he'd had a straw hat and a blade of corn between his teeth, Alex could never have imagined him actually farming anything.

The man grinned at him. "Hello, old chap!" he said.

"Hello, Mr Smithers," Alex replied.

Smithers worked for MI6. He had supplied the various devices Alex had used on his last mission.

"Very nice to see you again!" he exclaimed. He winked. "What do you think of the cover? I was told to blend in with the countryside."

"The combine harvester's a great idea," Alex

said. "Except this is April. There isn't anything to harvest."

"I hadn't thought of that!" Smithers beamed. "The trouble is, I'm not really a field agent. *Field* agent!" He looked around him and laughed. "Anyway, I'm jolly glad to have the chance to work with you again, Alex. To think up a few bits and pieces for you. It's not often I get a teenager. Much more fun than the adults!"

He reached into the cabin and pulled out a suitcase. "Actually, it's been a bit tricky this time," he went on.

"Have you got another Nintendo DS?" Alex asked.

"No. That's just it. The school doesn't allow games consoles, personal computers ... they won't even let you bring a mobile phone, so you can forget about the internet. It's a great shame. I could have hidden a dozen gadgets inside a laptop, but there you are! Now, let's see..." He opened the case. "I'm told there's still a lot of snow up at Point Blanc, so you'll need this."

"A ski suit," Alex said. That was what Smithers was holding.

"Yes. But it's highly insulated and also bullet-proof." He pulled out a pair of green-tinted goggles. "These are ski goggles. But in case you have to go anywhere at night, they're actually infrared. Just press the switch and you'll be able to see for about twenty metres, even if there's no moon. Oh, and by the way, I've popped a GPS receiver in the top pocket." He showed it to Alex. It was about the size of a watch with a digital display and a single button on the side. "GPS for Global Positioning System. Lots of skiers use them if they get lost off-piste but this one is a little different. It's a panic button. If the balloon goes up and you need help, just press the button three times. It'll send out a signal which our satellite will pick up. And then we come to the rescue."

Smither's reached into the case a third time. "One last thing. I must say, a skiing trip provides all sorts of possibilities," he continued. "Hand warmers!" He showed Alex half a dozen brightly coloured plastic packets. "But I wouldn't use them to warm your hands if I were you. Thirty seconds after you tear open the packet, they'll burn through anything."

"Thank you, Mr Smithers," Alex said. But he was disappointed and it showed.

Smithers understood. "I know what you want," he said, "but you know you can't have it. No guns! Mr Blunt is adamant. He thinks you're too young."

"Not too young to get killed though."

"Yes, well. I've given it a bit of thought and rustled up a couple of ... defensive measures, so to speak. This is just between you and me, you understand. I'm not sure Mr Blunt would approve."

He held out a hand. There was a gold ear-stud lying in two pieces in the middle of his palm; a diamond shape for the front and a catch to hold it at the back. The stud looked tiny surrounded by so much flesh. "They told me you'd had your ear pierced," he said. "So I made you this. Be very careful after you've put it in. Bringing the two pieces together will activate it."

"Activate what?" Alex looked doubtful.

"The ear-stud is a small but very powerful explosive device. Separating the two pieces again will set it off. Count to ten and it'll blow a hole in just about anything – or anyone, I should add."

"Just so long as it doesn't blow my ear off," Alex muttered.

"No, no. It's perfectly safe so long as the pieces remain attached." Smithers smiled. "And finally – I'm *very* pleased with this. It's exactly what you'd expect any young boy leaving for school to be given, and I bought it specially for you." He had produced a book.

Alex took it. It was a hardback edition of *Harry Potter and the Chamber of Secrets*. "Thanks," he said, "but I've already read it."

"This is a special edition. There's a gun built into the spine and the chamber is loaded with a stun dart. Just point it and press the author's name on the spine. It'll knock out an adult in less than five seconds."

Alex smiled. Smithers climbed back into the combine harvester. For a moment he seemed to have wedged himself permanently in the doorway, but then, with a grunt, he managed to go the whole way. "Good luck, old chap," he said. "Come back in one piece! I really do quite enjoy having you around!"

It was time to go.

Alex's luggage was being loaded into the helicopter and he was standing next to his "parents" clutching the Harry Potter book. Eva Stellenbosch was waiting for him beneath the rotors. He had been shocked by her appearance and at first he'd tried to hide it. But then he'd relaxed. He didn't have to be polite. Alex Rider might be well-mannered but Alex Friend wouldn't give a damn what she thought. He glanced at her scornfully now and noticed that she was watching him carefully as he said goodbye to the Friends.

Once again, Sir David Friend acted his part perfectly. "Goodbye, Alex," he said. "You will write to us and let us know you're OK?"

"If you want," Alex said.

Lady Caroline moved forward and kissed him. Alex backed away from her as if embarrassed. He had to admit that she looked genuinely sad.

"Come, Alex." Mrs Stellenbosch was in a hurry to get away. She told him that they would need to stop in Paris to refuel.

And then Fiona appeared, crossing the lawn towards them. Alex hadn't spoken to her since the business at the tunnel. Nor had she spoken to him. He had rejected her and he knew she would never forgive him. She hadn't come down to breakfast this morning and he'd assumed she wouldn't show herself again until he'd gone. So what was she doing here now?

Suddenly Alex knew. She'd come to cause trouble – one last jab below the belt. He could see it in her eyes and in the way she flounced across the lawn with her hands rolled into fists.

Fiona didn't know he was a spy. But she must know that he was here for a reason and she had probably guessed it had something to do with the woman from Point Blanc. So she had decided to come out and spoil things for him. Maybe she was going to ask questions. Maybe she was going to tell Mrs Stellenbosch that he wasn't really her brother. Either way, Alex knew that his mission would be over before it had even begun. All his work memorizing the files and all the time he had spent with the family would have been for nothing.

"Fiona!" Sir David muttered. His eyes were grave. He had come to the same conclusion as Alex.

She ignored him. "Are you here for Alex?" she asked, speaking directly to Mrs Stellenbosch.

"Yes, my dear."

"Well, I think there's something you should know."

There was only one thing Alex could do. He lifted the book and pointed it at Fiona, then pressed the spine once, hard. There was no noise, but he felt the book shudder in his hand. Fiona put her hand to the side of her leg. All the colour drained out of her face. She crumpled to the grass.

Lady Caroline ran over to her. Mrs Stellenbosch looked puzzled. Alex turned to her, his face blank. "That's my sister," he said. "She gets very emotional."

Two minutes later the helicopter took off. Alex

watched through the window as Haverstock Hall got smaller and smaller and then disappeared behind them. He looked at Mrs Stellenbosch hunched over the controls, her eyes hidden by her goggles. He eased himself into his seat and let himself be carried away into the darkening sky. Then the clouds rolled in. The countryside was gone. So was his only weapon. Alex was on his own.

ROOM 13

It was raining in Paris. The city was looking tired and disappointed, the Eiffel Tower fighting against a mass of heavy cloud. There was nobody sitting at the tables spread outside the cafés and for once the little kiosks selling paintings and postcards were being ignored by the tourists hurrying back to their hotels. It was five o'clock in the afternoon and the evening was drawing in. The shops and offices were emptying, but the city didn't care. It just wanted to be left alone.

The helicopter had landed in a private area of Charles de Gaulle airport and a car had been waiting to drive them in. Alex had said nothing during the flight and now he sat on his own in the back, watching the buildings flash by. They were following the Seine, moving surprisingly fast along a wide dual carriageway that dipped above and below the water level. Their route took them past Notre Dame. Then they turned off, weaving their way through a series of back streets with small restaurants and boutiques fighting for space on the pavements.

"The Marais," Mrs Stellenbosch said.

Alex pretended to show no interest. In fact, he had stayed in the Marais district once before and knew it as one of the smartest and most expensive quarters of Paris.

The car turned into a large square and stopped. Alex glanced out of the window. He was surrounded on four sides by the tall, classical houses for which Paris is famous. But the square had been disfigured by a single modern hotel. It was a white rectangular block, the windows fitted with dark glass that allowed no view to the inside. It rose up four floors, with a flat roof and the name HOTEL DU MONDE in gold letters above the main door. If a spaceship had landed in the square, crushing a couple of buildings to make room for itself, it couldn't have looked more out of place.

"This is where we're staying," Mrs Stellenbosch said. "The hotel is owned by the academy."

The driver had taken their cases out of the

boot. Alex followed the assistant director towards the entrance, the door sliding open automatically to allow them in. The reception was cold and faceless, white marble and mirrors, with a single potted plant tucked into a corner as an afterthought. There was a small reception desk with an unsmiling male receptionist in a dark suit and glasses, a computer and a row of pigeon holes. Alex counted them. There were fifteen. Presumably the hotel had fifteen rooms.

"*Bonsoir*, Madame Stellenbosch." The receptionist nodded his head slightly. He ignored Alex. "I hope you had a good journey from England," he continued, still speaking in French. Alex gazed blankly, as if he hadn't understood a word. Alex Friend wouldn't speak French. He wouldn't have bothered to learn. But Ian Rider had made certain that his nephew spoke French almost as soon as he spoke English. Not to mention German and Spanish as well.

The receptionist took down two keys. He didn't ask either of them to sign in. He didn't ask for a credit card. The school owned the hotel, so there would be no bill when they left. He gave Alex one of the keys.

"I hope you are not superstitious," he said, speaking in English now.

"No," Alex replied.

"It is room thirteen. On the first floor. I am sure you will find it most agreeable." The receptionist smiled.

Mrs Stellenbosch took her key. "The hotel has its own restaurant," she said. "We might as well eat here tonight. We don't want to go out in the rain. Anyway, the food here is excellent. Do you like French food, Alex?"

"Not much," Alex said.

"Well, I'm sure we'll find something that you like. Why don't you freshen up after the journey?" She looked at her watch. "We'll eat at seven. An hour and a half from now. It will give us an opportunity to talk together. Might I suggest, perhaps, some smarter clothes for dinner? The French are informal, but – if you'll forgive me saying so, my dear – you take informality a little far. I'll call you at five to seven. I hope the room is all right."

Room thirteen was at the end of a long, narrow corridor. The door opened into a surprisingly large space, with views over the square. There was a double bed with a black and white cover, a television and mini-bar, a desk and, on the wall, a couple of framed pictures of Paris. A porter had carried up Alex's cases and, as soon as he was gone, Alex kicked off his shoes and sat down on the bed. He wondered why they had come here. He knew the helicopter had needed refuelling, but that shouldn't have necessitated an overnight stop. Why not fly straight on to the school?

He had more than an hour to kill. First he went into the bathroom – more glass and white marble – and took a long shower. Then, wrapped in a towel, he went back into the room and put the television on. Alex Friend would watch a lot of television. There were about thirty channels to choose from. Alex skipped past the French ones and stopped on MTV. He wondered if he was being monitored. There was a large mirror next to the desk and it would have been easy enough to conceal a camera behind it. Well, why not give them something to think about? He opened the mini-bar and poured himself a glass of gin. Then he went into the bathroom, refilled the bottle with water and put it back in the fridge. Drinking alcohol and stealing! If she was watching, Mrs Stellenbosch would know that she had her hands full with him.

He spent the next forty minutes watching television and pretending to drink the gin. Then he took the glass into the bathroom and dumped it in the sink, allowing the liquid to run out. It was time to get dressed. Should he do what he was told and put on smart clothes? In the end, he compromised. He put on a shirt, but kept the same jeans. A moment later, the telephone rang. His call to dinner.

Mrs Stellenbosch was waiting for him in the restaurant, an airless room in the basement. Soft lighting and mirrors had been used to make it feel more spacious, but it was still the last place Alex would have chosen. The restaurant could have been anywhere, in any part of the world. There were two other diners – businessmen by the look of them – but otherwise they were alone. Mrs Stellenbosch had changed into a black evening dress with feathers at the collar and she wore an antique-looking necklace of black and silver beads. The smarter her clothes, Alex thought, the uglier she looked. She was smoking another cigar.

"Ah, Alex!" She blew smoke. "Did you have a rest? Or did you watch TV?"

Alex didn't say anything. He sat down and opened the menu, then closed it again when he saw that it was all in French.

"You must let me order for you. Some soup to start, perhaps? And then a steak. I've never yet met a boy who doesn't like steak."

"My cousin Oliver is a vegetarian," Alex said. It was something he had read in one of the files.

The assistant director nodded as if she already knew this. "Then he doesn't know what he is missing," she said. A pale-faced waiter came over and she placed the order in French. "What will you drink?" she asked.

"I'll have a Coke."

"A repulsive drink, I always think. I have never understood the taste. But, of course, you shall have what you want."

The waiter brought Alex a Coke and a glass of champagne for Mrs Stellenbosch. Alex watched the bubbles rising in the two glasses, his black, hers a pale gold.

"*Santé*," she said.

"I'm sorry?"

"It's French for 'good health'."

"Oh. Cheers."

There was a moment's silence. The woman's eyes were fixed on him – as if she could see right through him. "So, you were at Eton," she said casually.

"That's right." Alex was suddenly on his guard.

"What house were you in?"

"The Hopgarden." It was the name of a real

house at the school. Alex had read the file carefully.

"I visited Eton once. I remember a statue. I think it was a king. It was just through the main gate..."

She was testing him. Alex was sure of it. Did she suspect him – or was it simply a precaution, something she always did? "You're talking about Henry VI," he said. "His statue's in College Yard. He founded Eton."

"But you didn't like it there."

"No."

"Why not?"

"I didn't like the uniform and I didn't like the beaks." Alex was careful not to use the word "teachers". At Eton, they're known as beaks. He half smiled to himself. If she wanted a bit of Eton-speak, he'd give it to her. "And I didn't like the rules. Getting fined by the pop. Or being put in the tardy book. I was always getting rips and infoes or being put on the bill. The divs were boring—"

"I'm afraid I don't really understand a word you're saying."

"Divs are lessons," Alex explained. "Rips are when your work is no good—"

"All right!" She drew a line with her cigar. "Is

that why you set fire to the library?"

"No," Alex said. "That was just because I don't like books."

The first course arrived. Alex's soup was yellow and had something floating in it. He picked up his spoon and poked at it suspiciously. "What's this?" he demanded.

"*Soupe de moules.*"

He looked at her blankly.

"Mussel soup. I hope you enjoy it."

"I'd have preferred Heinz tomato," Alex said.

The steaks, when they came, were typically French; barely cooked at all. Alex took a couple of mouthfuls of the bloody meat, then threw down his knife and fork and used his fingers to eat the chips. Mrs Stellenbosch talked to him about the French Alps, about skiing and about her visits to various European cities. It was easy to look bored. He *was* bored. And he was beginning to feel tired. He took a sip of Coke, hoping the cold drink would wake him up. The meal seemed to be dragging on all night.

But at last the puddings – ice cream with white chocolate sauce – had come and gone. Alex declined coffee.

"You look tired," Stellenbosch said. She had lit another cigar. The smoke curled around her head and made him feel dizzy. "Would you like to go to bed?"

"Yes."

"We don't need to leave until midday tomorrow. You'll have time for a visit to the Louvre, if you'd like that."

Alex shook his head. "Actually, paintings bore me."

"Really? What a shame!"

Alex stood up. Somehow his hand knocked into his glass, spilling the rest of the Coke over the pristine white tablecloth. What was the matter with him? Suddenly he was exhausted.

"Would you like me to come up with you, Alex?" the woman asked. She was looking carefully at him, a tiny glimmer of interest in her otherwise dead eyes.

"No. I'll be all right." Alex stepped away. "Goodnight."

Getting upstairs was an ordeal. He was tempted to take the lift but he didn't want to lock himself into that small, windowless cubicle. He would have felt suffocated. He climbed the stairs, his shoulder resting heavily against the wall, stumbled down the corridor and somehow got the key into the lock. When he finally got inside, the room was spinning. What was going on? Had he drunk more of the gin than he had intended or was he...?

Alex swallowed. He had been drugged. There had been something in the Coke. It was still on his tongue, a sort of bitterness. There were only three steps between him and his bed, but it could have been a mile away. His legs wouldn't obey him any more. Just lifting one foot took all his strength. He fell forward, reaching out with his arms. Somehow he managed to propel himself far enough. His chest and shoulders hit the bed, sinking into the mattress. The room was spinning round him, faster and faster. He tried to stand up, tried to speak – but nothing came. His eyes closed. Gratefully, he allowed the darkness to take him.

Thirty minutes later, there was a soft click and the room began to change.

If Alex had been able to open his eyes, he would have seen the desk, the mini-bar and the framed pictures of Paris begin to rise up the wall. Or so it might have seemed to him. But in fact the walls weren't moving. The floor was sinking on hidden hydraulics, taking the bed – with Alex on it – into the depths of the hotel. The entire room was nothing more than a huge lift which was carrying him, one centimetre at a time, into the basement and beyond. Now the walls were metal sheets. He had left the wallpaper, the lights and the pictures high above him. He was dropping through what might have been a ventilation shaft with four steel rods guiding him to the bottom. Brilliant light suddenly flooded over him. There was another soft click. He had arrived.

The bed had come to rest in the centre of a gleaming underground clinic. Scientific equipment crowded in on him from all sides. There were a number of cameras – digital, video, infrared and X-ray. There were instruments of all shapes and sizes, many of them unrecognizable.

A tangle of wires spiralled out from each machine to a bank of computers that hummed and blinked on a long worktable against one of the walls. A window had been cut into the wall on the other side. The room was air-conditioned. Had Alex been awake, he might have shivered in the cold. His breath appeared as a faint white cloud hovering around his mouth.

A plump man wearing a white coat was waiting to receive him. The man was about forty, with yellow hair slicked back and a face that was rapidly sinking into middle-age, with puffy cheeks and a thick, fatty neck. The man had glasses and a small moustache. He had two assistants with him. They were also wearing white coats. Their faces were blank.

The three of them set to work at once. Handling Alex as if he were a sack of vegetables – or a corpse – they picked him up and stripped off all his clothes. Then they began to photograph him, using a conventional camera to begin with. Starting at his toes, they moved upwards, clicking off at least a hundred pictures, the flash igniting and the film automatically spooling forward. Not one inch of his body escaped their examination. A lock of his hair was snipped off and slid into a plastic envelope. An opthalmoscope was used to produce a perfect image of the back of his eye. They made a moulding of his teeth, slipping a piece of putty into his mouth and manipulating his chin to make him bite down. They made a careful note of the birthmark on his left shoulder, the scar on his arm and even his fingerprints. Alex bit his nails. That was recorded too.

Finally, they weighed him on a large, flat scale and then measured him – his height, chest, waist, inside leg, hand size and so on – making a note of every measurement on clipboards.

And all the time, Mrs Stellenbosch watched from the other side of the window. She never moved. The only sign of life anywhere in her face was the cigar, clamped between her lips. It glowed red and the smoke trickled up.

The three men had finished. The one with the yellow hair spoke into a microphone. "We're all done," he said.

"Give me your opinion, Mr Baxter." The woman's voice echoed out of a concealed speaker.

"It's a cinch." The man called Baxter was English. He spoke with an upper-class accent. And he was obviously pleased with himself. "He's got a good bone structure. Very fit. Interesting face. You notice the pierced ear? He's had that done recently. Nothing else to say, really."

"When will you operate?"

"Whenever you say, old girl. Just let me know."

Mrs Stellenbosch turned to the other two men. *"Rhabillez-le!"* She snapped the two words.

The two assistants put Alex's clothes back on him again. This took longer than taking them off. As they worked, they made a careful note of all the brand names. The Levi shirt, the Paul Smith socks. By the time they had dressed him, they knew as much about him as a doctor knows about a newborn baby. It had all been noted down. And the information would be passed on.

Mr Baxter walked over to the worktable and

pressed a button. At once, the carpet, bed and hotel furniture began to rise up. They disappeared through the ceiling and kept going. Alex slept on as he was carried back up the shaft, finally arriving in the space that he knew as room thirteen.

There was nothing to show what had happened. The whole experience had evaporated, as quickly as a dream.

"MY NAME IS GRIEF"

The academy at Point Blanc had been built by a lunatic. For a time it had been used as an asylum. Alex remembered what Alan Blunt had told him as the helicopter began its final descent, the red and white helipad looming up to receive it. The photograph in the brochure had been artfully taken. Now that he could see the building for himself, he could only describe it as ... mad.

It was a jumble of towers and battlements, green sloping roofs and windows of every shape and size. Nothing fitted together properly. The overall design should have been simple enough; a circular central area with two wings. But one wing was longer than the other. The two sides didn't match. The academy was four floors high but the windows were spaced in such a way that it was hard to tell where one floor ended and the next began. There was an internal courtyard that wasn't quite square, with a fountain that had frozen solid. Even the helipad, jutting out of the roof, was ugly and awkward, as if a spaceship had smashed into the brickwork and lodged in place.

Mrs Stellenbosch flicked off the controls. "I will take you down to meet the director," she shouted over the noise of the blades. "Your luggage will be brought down later."

It was cold on the roof, the snow covering the mountain still hadn't melted and everything was white for as far as the eye could see.

The academy was built into the side of a steep slope. A little further down, Alex saw a great iron tongue that started at ground level but then curved outwards as the mountainside dropped away. It was a ski-jump – the sort of thing he had seen at the Winter Olympics. The end of the curve was at least fifty metres above the ground and, far below, Alex could make out a flat area shaped like a horseshoe where the jumpers were meant to land.

He was staring at it, imagining what it would be like to propel yourself into space with only two skis to break your fall, when the woman grabbed his arm. "We don't use it," she said. "It is forbidden.

Come now. Let's get out of the cold."

They went through a door in the side of one of the towers and down a narrow spiral staircase – each step a different distance apart – that took them all the way to the ground floor. Now they were in a long, narrow corridor with plenty of doors but no windows.

"Classrooms," Mrs Stellenbosch explained. "You will see them later."

Alex followed her through the strangely silent building. The central heating had been turned up high inside the academy and the atmosphere was warm and heavy. They stopped at a pair of modern glass doors which opened into the courtyard that Alex had seen from above. From the heat back into the cold again, Mrs Stellenbosch led him through the doors and past the frozen fountain. A movement caught his eye and Alex glanced up. This was something he hadn't noticed earlier. A sentry stood on one of the towers. He had a pair of binoculars round his neck and a submachine-gun slung across one arm.

Armed guards? In a school? Alex had only been here a few minutes and already he was unnerved.

"Through here." Mrs Stellenbosch opened another door for him and he found himself in the main reception hall of the academy. A log fire was burning in a massive fireplace with two stone dragons guarding the flames. A grand staircase led upwards. The hall was lit by a chandelier with at least a hundred bulbs. The walls were wood panelled. The carpet was thick, dark red. A dozen pairs of eyes pursued Alex as he followed Mrs Stellenbosch towards the next corridor. The hall was decorated with animal heads. A rhino, an antelope, a water buffalo and, saddest of all, a lion. Alex wondered who had shot them.

They came to a single door, which suggested they had come to the end of their journey. So far Alex hadn't encountered any boys but, glancing out of the window, he saw two more guards marching slowly past, both of them cradling machine-guns.

Mrs Stellenbosch knocked on the door.

"Come in!" Even with just two words, Alex caught the South African accent.

The door opened and they went into a huge room that made no sense. Like the rest of the building, its shape was irregular, none of the walls running parallel. The ceiling was about seven metres high, with windows running the whole way and giving an impressive view of the slopes. The room was modern, with soft lighting coming from units concealed in the walls. The furniture was ugly, but not as ugly as the further animal heads on the walls and the zebra skin on the wooden floor. There were three chairs next to a small fireplace. One of them was gold and antique. A man was sitting in it. His head turned as Alex came in.

"Good afternoon, Alex," he said. "Please come and sit down."

Alex sauntered into the room and took one of the chairs. Mrs Stellenbosch sat in the other.

"My name is Grief," the man continued. "Dr Grief. I am very pleased to meet you and to have you here."

Alex stared at the man who was the director of Point Blanc, at the white paper skin and the eyes burning behind the red spectacles. It was like meeting a skeleton and for a moment he was lost for words. Then he recovered. "Nice place," he said.

"Do you think so?" There was no emotion whatsoever in Grief's voice. So far he had moved only his neck. "This building was designed in 1857 by a Frenchman who was certainly the world's worst architect. This was his only commission. When the first owners moved in, they had him shot."

"There are still quite a few people here with

guns." Alex glanced out of the window as another pair of guards walked past.

"Point Blanc is unique," Dr Grief explained. "As you will soon discover, all the boys who have been sent here come from families of great wealth and importance. We have had the sons of emperors and industrialists. Boys like yourself. It follows that we could very easily become a target for terrorists. The guards are therefore here for your protection."

"That's very kind of you." Alex felt he was being too polite. It was time to show this man what sort of person he was meant to be. "But to be honest, I don't really want to be here myself. So if you'll just tell me how I get down into town, maybe I can get the next train home."

"There is no way down into town." Dr Grief lifted a hand to stop Alex interrupting. Alex looked at his long, skeletal fingers and at the eyes glinting red behind the spectacles. The man moved as if every bone in his body had been broken and then put back together again; he seemed both old and young at the same time and somehow not completely human. "The skiing season is over ... it's too dangerous now. There is only the helicopter and that will take you from here only when I say so." The hand lowered itself again. "You are here, Alex, because you have disappointed your parents. You were expelled from school. You have had difficulties with the police—"

"That wasn't my bloody fault!" Alex protested.

"Don't interrupt the doctor!" Mrs Stellenbosch said.

Alex glanced at her balefully.

"Your appearance is displeasing," Dr Grief went on. "Your language also. It is our job to turn you into a boy of whom your parents can be proud."

"I'm happy as I am," Alex said.

"That is of no relevance." Dr Grief fell silent.

Alex shivered. There was something about this room; so big, so empty, so twisted out of shape. "So what are you going to do with me?" Alex asked.

"There will be no lessons to begin with," Mrs Stellenbosch said. "For the first couple of weeks we want you to assimilate."

"What does that mean?"

"To assimilate. To conform ... to adapt ... to become like." It was as if she were reading out of a dictionary. "There are six boys at the academy at the moment. You will meet them and you will spend time with them. There will be opportunities for sport and for being social.

There is a good library here and you will read. Soon, you will learn our methods."

"I want to call my mum and dad," Alex said.

"The use of telephones is forbidden," Mrs Stellenbosch explained. She tried to smile sympathetically, but with *her* face it wasn't quite possible. "We find it makes our students homesick," she went on. "Of course, you may write letters if you wish."

"I prefer e-mails," Alex said.

"For the same reason, personal computers are not permitted."

Alex shrugged, and swore under his breath.

Dr Grief had seen him. "You will be polite to the assistant director!" he snapped. He hadn't raised his voice but the words came out acid. "You should be aware, Alex, that Mrs Stellenbosch has worked with me now for twenty-six years and that when I met her she had been voted Miss South Africa five years in a row."

Alex looked at the ape-like face. "A beauty contest?" he asked.

"The weightlifting championships." Dr Grief glanced at the fireplace. "Show him," he said.

Mrs Stellenbosch got up and went over to the fireplace. There was a poker lying in the grate. She took it with both hands. For a moment she seemed to concentrate. Alex gasped. The solid metal poker, at least two centimetres thick, was slowly bending. Now it was u-shaped. Mrs Stellenbosch wasn't even sweating. She brought the two ends together and dropped it back into the grate. It clanged against the stone.

"We enforce strict discipline here at the academy," Dr Grief said. "Bedtime is at ten o'clock – not a minute past. We do not tolerate bad language. You will have no contact with the outside world without our permission. You will not attempt to leave. And you will do as you are told instantly, without hesitation. And finally" – he leaned towards Alex – "you are permitted only in certain parts of this building." He gestured with a hand and for the first time Alex noticed a second door at the far end of the room. "My private quarters are through there. You will remain on the ground floor and the first floor only. That is where the bedrooms and classrooms are located. The second and third floors are out of bounds. The basement also. This is again for your safety."

"You're afraid I'll trip on the stairs?" Alex asked.

Dr Grief ignored him. "You may leave," he said.

"Wait outside the office, Alex," Mrs Stellenbosch said. "Someone will be along to collect you."

Alex stood up.

"We will make you into what your parents want," Dr Grief said.

"Maybe they don't want me at all."

"We can arrange that too."

Alex went.

"An unpleasant boy ... a few days ... faster than usual ... the Gemini Project ... closing down..."

If the door hadn't been so thick, Alex would have been able to hear more. The moment he had left the room he'd cupped his ear against the keyhole, hoping to pick up something that might be useful to MI6. Sure enough, Dr Grief and Mrs Stellenbosch were busily talking on the other side, but Alex heard little and understood less.

A hand clamped down on his shoulder and he twisted round, annoyed with himself. A so-called spy caught listening at the keyhole! But it wasn't one of the guards. Alex found himself looking up at a round-faced boy with long dark hair, dark eyes and pale skin. He was wearing a very old *Star Wars* T-shirt, torn jeans and a baseball cap. Recently he had been in a fight, and it looked like he'd got the worst of it. There was a bruise around one of his eyes and a gash on his lip.

"They'll shoot you if they catch you listening at doors," the boy said. He looked at Alex with hostile eyes. Alex guessed he was the sort of boy who wouldn't trust anyone easily. "I'm James Sprintz," he said. "They told me to show you round."

"Alex Friend."

"So what did you do to get sent to this dump?" James asked as they walked back down the corridor.

"I got expelled from Eton."

"I got thrown out of a school in Düsseldorf." James sighed. "I thought it was the best thing that ever happened to me. Until my dad sent me here."

"What does your dad do?" Alex asked.

"He's a banker. He plays the money markets. He loves money and has lots of it." James's voice was flat, unemotional.

"Dieter Sprintz?" Alex remembered the name. He'd made the front page of every newspaper in England a few years before. The One Hundred Million Dollar Man. That was how much he had made in just twenty-four hours. At the same time the pound had crashed and the British government had almost collapsed.

"Yeah. Don't ask me to show you a photograph

because I don't have one. This way."

They had reached the main hall with the dragon fireplace. From here, James showed him to the dining-room, a long, high-ceilinged room with six tables and a hatch leading into the kitchen. After that, they visited two living-rooms, a games room and a library. The academy reminded Alex of an expensive hotel in a ski resort – and not just because of its setting. There was a sort of heaviness about the place, a sense of being cut off from the real world. The air was warm and silent and, despite the size of the rooms, Alex couldn't help feeling claustro-phobic. If the place *had* been a hotel, it would have been an unpopular one. Grief had said there were only six boys living there. The build-ing could have housed sixty. Empty space was everywhere.

There was nobody in either of the living-rooms – just a collection of armchairs, desks and tables – but they found a couple of boys in the library. This was a long, narrow room with old-fashioned oak shelves lined with books in a vari-ety of languages. A suit of medieval Swiss armour stood in an alcove at the far end.

"This is Tom. And Hugo," James said. "They're probably doing extra maths or something, so we'd better not disturb them."

The two boys looked up and nodded briefly. One of them was reading a textbook. The other was writing. They were both much more smartly dressed than James and didn't look very friendly.

"Creeps," James said as soon as they had left the room.

"In what way?"

"When I was told about this place, they said *all* the kids had problems. I thought it was going to be wild. Do you have a cigarette?"

"I don't smoke."

"Great. I get here and it's like a museum or a monastery or ... I don't know what. It looks like Dr Grief's been busy. Everyone's quiet, hard-working, boring. God knows how he did it. Sucked their brains out with a straw or something. A couple of days ago I got into a fight with a couple of them, just for the hell of it." He pointed to his face. "They beat the crap out of me and then went back to their studies. Really creepy!"

They went into the games room, which contained table tennis, darts, a wide-screen TV and a snooker table. "Don't try playing snooker," James said. "The room's on a slant and all the balls roll to the side."

Then they went upstairs. This was where

the boys had their study bedrooms. Each one contained a bed, an armchair, a television ("It only shows the programmes Dr Grief wants you to see," James said), a wardrobe and a desk, with a second door leading into a small bathroom with a toilet and shower. None of the rooms were locked.

"We're not allowed to lock them," James explained. "We're all stuck here with nowhere to go, so nobody bothers to steal anything. Hugo Vries – the boy in the library – used to nick anything he could get his hands on. He was arrested for shoplifting in Amsterdam."

"But not any more?"

"He's another success story. He's flying home next week. His father owns diamond mines. Why bother shoplifting when you can afford to buy the whole shop?"

Alex's study was at the end of the corridor, with views over the ski-jump. His suitcases had already been carried up and were waiting for him on the bed. Everything felt very bare but, according to James, the study bedrooms were the only part of the school which the boys were allowed to decorate themselves. They could choose their own duvets and cover the walls with their own posters.

"They say it's important that you express yourself," James said. "If you haven't brought anything with you, Miss Stomach-bag will take you into Grenoble."

"Miss Stomach-bag?"

"Mrs Stellenbosch. That's my name for her."

"What do the other boys call her?"

"They call her Mrs Stellenbosch." James paused by the door. "This is a deeply weird place, Alex. I've been to a lot of schools because I've been thrown out of a lot of schools. But this one is the pits. I've been here for six weeks now and I've hardly had any lessons. They have music evenings and discussion evenings and they try to get me to read. But otherwise I've been left on my own."

"They want you to assimilate," Alex said, remembering what Dr Grief had said.

"That's *their* word for it. But this place ... they may call it a school, but it's more like being in prison. You've seen the guards."

"I thought they were here to protect us."

"If you think that, you're a bigger idiot than I thought. Think about it! There are about thirty of them. Thirty armed guards for seven kids. That's not protection. That's intimidation." James examined Alex for a second time. "It would be nice to think that someone has finally arrived

151

who I can relate to," he said.

"Maybe you can," Alex said.

"Yeah. But for how long?"

James left, closing the door behind him.

Alex began to unpack. The bullet-proof ski suit and infrared goggles were at the top of the first case. It didn't look as if he would be needing them. It wasn't as if he even had any skis. He found the hand warmers in their brightly coloured packets and laid them aside. Then came the GPS receiver with the panic button built into the side. He remembered the instructions Smithers had given him. "If the balloon goes up, just press the button three times." He was almost tempted to do it now. There was something unsettling about the academy. He could feel it even now, in his room. He was like a goldfish in a bowl. Looking up, he almost expected to see a pair of huge eyes looming over him and he knew that they would be wearing red-tinted glasses. He weighed the little device in his hand. He couldn't hit the panic button – not yet. He had nothing to report back to MI6. There was nothing to connect the school with the deaths of the two men in New York and the Black Sea.

But if there was anything, he knew where he would find it. Why were two whole floors of the building out of bounds? Presumably the guards slept up there but even though Dr Grief seemed to employ a small army, that would still leave a lot of empty rooms. The second and third floors. If something was going on at the academy, it had to be going on there.

A bell sounded downstairs. Alex swung his case shut, left his room and walked down the corridor. He saw another couple of boys walking ahead of him, talking quietly together. Like the boys he had seen in the library, they were both clean and well-dressed, with hair cut short and smartly groomed. Majorly creepy, James had said. Even on first sight, Alex had to agree.

He reached the main staircase. The two boys had gone down. Alex glanced in their direction, then went up. The staircase turned a corner and stopped. Ahead of him was a sheet of metal that rose up from the floor to the ceiling and all the way across, blocking off the view. The wall had been added recently, like the helipad. Someone had carefully and deliberately cut the building in two.

There was a door set in the metal wall and beside it a key pad with nine buttons demanding a code. Alex reached for the door handle, his hand closing around it. He didn't expect the door to open – but nor did he expect what happened next. The moment his fingers came into contact with the handle, an alarm went off, a shrieking siren that echoed throughout the building. A few seconds later he became aware of footsteps on the stairs and turned to find two guards facing him, their guns raised.

Neither of them spoke to him. One of them pushed past him and punched a code into the key pad. The alarm stopped. And then Mrs Stellenbosch was there, hurrying forward on her short, stubby legs.

"Alex!" she exclaimed. Her eyes were filled with suspicion. "What are you doing here? The director told you that the upper floors are forbidden."

"Yeah ... well I forgot." Alex looked straight at her. "I heard the bell go and I was on my way to the dining-room."

"The dining-room is downstairs."

"Right."

Alex walked past the two guards, who stepped aside to let him pass. He felt Mrs Stellenbosch watching him as he went. Metal doors, alarms and guards with machine-guns. What were they hiding? And then he remembered something else. The Gemini Project. Those were the words he had heard when he was listening at Dr Grief's door.

Gemini. The twins. One of the twelve star signs.
But what did it mean?

Turning the question over in his mind, Alex went down to meet the rest of the school.

THINGS THAT GO CLICK IN THE NIGHT

At the end of his first week at Point Blanc, Alex drew up a list of the six boys with whom he shared the school. It was mid-afternoon and he was alone in his room. There was a note-pad open in front of him. It had taken him about half an hour to put together the names and the few details that he had. He only wished he had more.

HUGO VRIES (14) Dutch, lives in Amsterdam. Brown hair, green eyes. Father's name: Rudi, owns diamond mines. Speaks little English. Reads and plays guitar. Very solitary. Sent to PB for shoplifting and arson.

TONY McMORIN (14) Canadian, from Vancouver. Parents divorced. Mother runs media empire (newspapers, TV). Reddish hair, blue eyes. Well-built, chess player. Car thefts and drunken driving.

NICOLAS MARC (14) French, from Bordeaux? Expelled from private School in Paris, cause unknown - drinking? Brown hair, brown eyes, very fit all-rounder. Good at sport but hates losing. Tattoo of devil on left shoulder. Father: Anthony Marc - airlines, pop music, hotels. Never mentions his mother

CASSIAN JAMES (14) American.
Fair hair, brown eyes. Mother: Jill,
studio chief in Hollywood. Parents
divorced. Loud voice. Swears a lot.
Plays jazz piano. Expelled from
three schools. Various drug offences
-sent to PB after smuggling
arrest but won't talk about it
now. One of the kids who beat
up James. Stronger than he looks.

JOE CANTERBURY (14) American.
Spends a lot of his time with Cassian.
(helped him with James). Brown
hair, blue eyes. Mother (name
unknown) New York senator. Father
Something big at the Pentagon.
Vandalism, truancy, shoplifting. Sent
to PB after stealing and
smashing up car. Vegetarian.
Permanently chewing gum. Has
he given up smoking?

JAMES SPRINTZ (14) German, lives in Düsseldorf. Brown hair, brown eyes, pale. Father: Dieter Sprintz, banker, well-known financier (the One Hundred Million Dollar Man). Mother living in England. Expelled for wounding a teacher with an air-pistol. My only friend at PB! And the only one who really hates it here.

Lying on his bed, Alex studied the list. What did it tell him? Not a great deal.

First, all the boys were the same age – fourteen. The same age as him. At least three of them, and possibly four, had parents who were either divorced or separated. They all came from hugely wealthy backgrounds. Blunt had already told him that was the case, but Alex was surprised by just how diverse the parents were. Airlines, diamonds, politics and movies. France, Germany, Holland, Canada and America. All of the parents were at the top of his or her field and those fields covered just about every human activity.

159

He himself was supposed to be the son of a super-market king. Food. That was another world indus-try he could tick off.

At least two of the boys had been arrested for shoplifting. Two of them had been involved with drugs. But Alex knew that the list somehow hid more than it revealed. With the exception of James, it was hard to pin down what made the boys at Point Blanc different. In a strange way, they all looked the same.

Their eyes and hair were different colours. They wore different clothes. All the faces were differ-ent: Tom handsome and confident, Joe quiet and watchful. And of course they spoke not only with different voices but in several languages. James had talked about brains being sucked out with straws and he had a point. It was as if the same consciousness had somehow invaded them all. They had become puppets dancing on the same string.

The bell rang downstairs. Alex looked at his watch. It was exactly one o'clock – lunch-time. That was another thing about the school. Every-thing was done to the exact minute. Lessons from nine until twelve. Lunch from one to two. And so on. James made a point of being late for every-thing and Alex had taken to joining him. It was

a tiny rebellion, but a satisfying one. It showed
they still had a little control over their lives. The
other boys, of course, turned up like clockwork.
They would be in the dining-room now, waiting
quietly for the food to be served.

Alex rolled over on the bed and reached for
a pen. He wrote a single word on the pad, underneath the names.

Brainwashing?

Maybe that was the answer. According to James,
the other boys had arrived at the academy two
months before him. He had been there for six
weeks. That added up to just fourteen weeks in
total and Alex knew that you didn't take a bunch
of delinquents and turn them into perfect students just by giving them good books. Dr Grief
had to be doing something else. Drugs? Hypnosis?
Something.

He waited five more minutes, then hid the
note-pad under his mattress and left the room.
He wished he could lock the door. There was no
privacy at Point Blanc. Even the bathrooms had
no locks. And Alex still couldn't shake off the feeling that everything he did, even everything he

thought, was somehow being monitored, noted down. Evidence to be used against him.

It was ten past one when he reached the dining-room and, sure enough, the other boys were already there, eating their lunch and talking quietly amongst themselves. Nicolas and Cassian were at one table. Hugo, Tom and Joe were at another. Nobody was flicking peas. Nobody even had their elbows on the table. Tom was talking about a visit he had made to some museum in Grenoble. Alex had only been in the room for a few seconds but already his appetite had gone.

James had arrived just ahead of him and was standing at the hatch, helping himself to food. Most of the food arrived pre-cooked and one of the guards heated it up. Today it was stew. Alex got his lunch and sat next to James. The two of them had their own table. They had become friends quite effortlessly. Everyone else ignored them.

"You want to go out after lunch?" James asked.

"Sure. Why not?"

"There's something I want to talk to you about."

Alex looked past James at the other boys. There was Tom, at the head of the table, reaching out for a jug of water. He was dressed in a polo jersey and jeans. Next to him was Joe Canterbury, the American. He was talking to Hugo now, waving a finger to emphasize a point. Where had Alex seen that movement before? Cassian was just behind them, round-faced, with fine, light brown hair, laughing at a joke.

Different but the same. Watching them closely, Alex tried to work out what that meant.

It was all in the details, the things you wouldn't notice unless you saw them all together like they were now. The way they were all sitting with their backs straight and their elbows close to their sides. The way they held their knives and forks. Hugo laughed and Alex realized that for a moment he had become a mirror image of Cassian. It was the same laugh. He watched Joe eat a mouthful of food. Then he watched Nicolas. They were two different boys. There was no doubting that. But they ate in the same way, as if they were mimicking each other.

There was a movement at the door and suddenly Mrs Stellenbosch appeared. "Good afternoon, boys," she said.

"Good afternoon, Mrs Stellenbosch." Five people answered, but Alex heard only one voice. He and James remained silent.

"Lessons this afternoon will begin at three o'clock. The subjects will be Latin and French."

The lessons would be taught by Dr Grief or Mrs Stellenbosch. There were no other teachers at the school. Alex hadn't yet been taught anything. James dipped in and out of class, depending on his mood.

"There will be a discussion this evening in the library," Mrs Stellenbosch went on. "The subject is 'violence in television and film'. Mr McMorin will be opening the debate. Afterwards there will be hot chocolate and Dr Grief will be giving a lecture on the works of Mozart. Everyone is welcome to attend."

James jabbed a finger into his open mouth and stuck out his tongue. Alex smiled. The other boys were listening quietly.

"Dr Grief would also like to congratulate Cassian James on winning the poetry competition. His poem is pinned to the notice-board in the main hall. That is all."

She turned and left the room. James rolled his eyes. "Let's go out and get some fresh air," he said. "I'm feeling sick."

The two of them went upstairs and put on their coats. James had the room next door to Alex and had done his best to make it more homely. There were posters of Batman movies on the walls and a mobile of the solar system dangling above the bed. A red and white Tintin space rocket stood on the bedside table next to a photograph of two people, presumably his parents. There were clothes everywhere. James obviously didn't believe in hanging them up. Somehow he managed to find a scarf and a single glove. He shoved one hand into a pocket. "Let's go!" he said.

They went back down and along the corridor, passing the games room. Nicolas and Cassian were playing table tennis and Alex stopped at the door to watch them. The ball was bouncing back and forth and Alex found himself mesmerized. He stood there for about sixty seconds, watching. Kerplink, kerplunk, kerplink, kerplunk – neither of the boys were scoring. There it was again. Different but the same. Obviously there were two boys there. But the way they played, the style of their game, was identical. If it had been one boy, knocking a ball up against a mirror, the result would have looked much the same. Alex shivered. James was standing at his shoulder. The two of them moved away.

Hugo was sitting in the library. The boy who had been sent to Point Blanc for shoplifting was reading a Dutch edition of *National Geographic* magazine. They reached the hall and there was

Cassian's poem, prominently pinned to the notice-board. He had been sent to Point Blanc for smuggling drugs. Now he was writing about daffodils.

Alex pushed open the main door and felt the cold wind hit his face. He was grateful for it. He needed to be reminded that there was a real world outside.

It had begun to snow again. The two boys walked slowly round the building. A couple of guards walked towards them, speaking softly in German. Alex had counted thirty guards at Point Blanc, all of them young German men, dressed in uniform black roll-neck sweaters and black padded waistcoats. The guards never spoke to the boys. They had pale, unhealthy faces and close-cropped hair. Dr Grief had said they were there for his protection, but Alex still wondered. Were they there to keep intruders out – or the boys in?

"This way," James said.

James walked ahead, his feet sinking into the thick snow. Alex followed, looking back at the windows on the second and third floors. It was maddening. Half of the castle – perhaps more – was closed off to him and he still couldn't think of a way of getting up there. He couldn't climb. The brickwork was too smooth and there was no convenient ivy to provide handholds. The drainpipes looked too fragile to take his weight.

Something moved. Alex stopped in his tracks.

"What is it?" James asked.

"There!" Alex pointed at the third floor. He thought he'd seen a figure watching them from a window two floors above his room. It was only there for a moment. The face seemed to be covered – a white mask with narrow slits for the eyes. But even as he pointed, the figure stepped back, out of sight.

"I don't see anything," James said.

"It's gone."

They walked on, heading for the abandoned ski-jump. According to James, the jump had been built just before Grief had bought the academy. There had been plans to turn the building into a winter sports training centre. The jump had never been used. They reached the wooden barriers that lay across the entrance and stopped.

"Let me ask you something," James said. His breath was misting in the cold air. "What do you think of this place?"

"Why do we have to talk out here?" Alex asked. Despite his coat, he was beginning to shiver.

"Because when I'm inside the building, I get the feeling that someone is listening to every word I say."

Alex nodded. "I know what you mean." He considered the question James had put to him. "I think you were right the first day we met," he said. "This place is creepy."

"So how would you feel about getting out of here?"

"You know how to fly the helicopter?"

"No. But I'm going." James paused and looked around. The two guards had gone into the school. There was nobody else in sight. "I can trust you, Alex, because you've only just got here. He hasn't got to you yet." *He* was Dr Grief. James didn't need to say the name. "But believe me," he went on, "it won't be long. If you stay here, you're going to end up like the others. Model students – that's exactly the term for them. It's like they're all made out of Plasticene! Well, I've had enough. I'm not going to let him do that to me!"

"Are you going to run away?" Alex asked.

"Who needs to run?" James looked down the slope. "I'm going to ski."

Alex looked at the slope. It plunged steeply down, stretching on for ever. "Is that possible?" he asked. "I thought—"

"I know Grief says it's too dangerous. But he

would, wouldn't he. It's true it's black runs all the way down and there'll be tons of moguls—"

"Won't the snow have melted?"

"Only further down." James pointed. "I've been right down to the bottom," he said. "I did it the first week I was here. All the slopes run into a single valley. It's called La Vallée de Fer. You can't actually make it as far as the town because there's a train track that cuts across. But if I can get to the track, I reckon I can walk the rest of the way."

"And then?"

"A train back to Düsseldorf. If my dad tries to send me back here, I'll go to my mum in England. If she doesn't want me, I'll disappear. I've got friends in Paris and Berlin. I don't care. All I know is, I've got to split and if you know what's good for you, you'll come too."

Alex considered. He was tempted to join the other boy, if only to help him on his way. But he had a job to do. "I don't have any skis," he said.

"Nor do I." James spat into the snow. "Grief took all the skis when the season ended. He's got them locked up somewhere."

"On the third floor?"

"Maybe. But I'll find them. And then I'm out of here." He reached out to Alex with his ungloved hand. "Come with me."

Alex shook his head. "I'm sorry, James. You go, and good luck to you. But I'll stick it out a bit longer. I don't want to break my neck."

"OK. That's your lookout. I'll send you a postcard."

The two of them walked back towards the school. Alex gestured at the window where he had seen the masked face. "Have you ever wondered what goes on up there?" he asked.

"No." James shrugged. "I suppose that's where the guards live."

"Two whole floors?"

"There's a basement as well. And Dr Grief's rooms. Do you think he sleeps with Miss Stomach-bag?" James made a face. "That's a pretty gross thought, the two of them together. Darth Vader and King Kong. Well, I'm going to find my skis and get out of here, Alex. And if you've got any sense, you'll come too."

Alex and James were skiing together down the slope, the blades cutting smoothly through the surface snow. It was a perfect night. Everything frozen and still. They had left the academy behind them. But then Alex saw a figure ahead of them. Dr Grief was there! He was standing motionless,

170

wearing his dark suit, his eyes quite hidden by his red-lensed spectacles. Alex veered away from him. He lost control. He was moving faster and faster down the slope, his poles flailing at the air, his skis refusing to turn. He could see the ski-jump ahead of him. Someone had removed the barriers. He felt his skis leave the snow and shoot forward onto solid ice. And then it was a screaming drop down, tearing ever further into the night, knowing there was no way back. Dr Grief laughed and at the same moment there was a click and Alex shot into space, spinning a mile above the ground and then falling, falling, falling...

He woke up.

He was lying in bed, the moonlight spilling onto the covers. He looked at his watch. Two-fifteen. He played back the dream he had just had. Trying to escape with James. Dr Grief waiting for them. He had to admit, the academy was beginning to get to him. He didn't usually have bad dreams. But the school and the people in it were slipping under his skin, working their way into his mind.

He thought about what he had heard. Dr Grief laughing – and something else ... a clicking sound. That was strange. What had gone "click"?

Had it actually been part of the dream? Suddenly Alex was completely awake. He got out of bed, went to the door and turned the handle. He was right. He hadn't imagined the sound. While he was asleep, the door had been locked from outside.

Something had to be happening – and Alex was determined to see what it was. He got dressed as quickly as possible, then knelt down and examined the lock. He could make out two bolts, at least a centimetre in diameter, one at the top and one at the bottom. They must have been activated automatically. One thing was sure. He wasn't going to get out through the door.

That left the window. All the bedroom windows were fastened with a steel rod that allowed them to open ten centimetres but no more. Alex picked up one of the hand warmers and tore open the plastic cover. Inside, there was a strip of what looked like grey putty. He remembered what Smithers had told him. He had thirty seconds before it activated. Alex wrapped the putty around the steel rod, then stood back. A wisp of smoke suddenly rose into the air and at the same time he heard a fierce hissing sound as the chemical – whatever it was – burned through the metal. The rod fell apart, allowing the window to swing fully open.

It was snowing. Alex put away the other hand

warmers – he might need them later. Then he pulled on his coat and climbed out of the window. He was one floor up. Normally a fall from that height would have broken an ankle or a leg. But it had been snowing for the best part of ten hours and a white bank had built up against the wall right beneath him. Alex lowered himself as far as he could, then let go. He fell through the air and hit the snow, disappearing as far as his waist. He was freezing and damp before he had even started. But he was unhurt.

He climbed out of the snow and began to move round the side of the building, making for the front. He would just have to hope that the main entrance wasn't locked too. But somehow he was sure it wouldn't be. His door had been locked automatically. Presumably a switch had been thrown and all the others had been locked too. Most of the boys would be asleep. Even the ones who were awake wouldn't be going anywhere, leaving Dr Grief free to do whatever he wanted, coming and going as he pleased.

Alex had just made it to the side of the building when he heard the guards approach, boots crunching. There was nowhere to hide so he threw himself face-down into the snow, hugging the shadows. There were two of them. He could hear them talking softly in German but he didn't dare look up. If he made any movement, they would see him. If they came too close, they would probably see him anyway. He held his breath, his heart pounding.

The guards walked past and round the corner. Their path would take them under his room. Would they see the open window? Alex had left the light off. Hopefully there would be no reason for them to look up. But he was still aware that he might not have much time. He had to move – now.

He lifted himself up and ran forward. His clothes were covered in snow and more flakes were falling, drifting into his eyes. It was the coldest part of the night and Alex was shivering by the time he reached the main door. What would he do if it was locked after all? He certainly wouldn't be able to stay out in the open until morning.

But the door was unlocked. Alex pushed it open and slipped into the warmth and darkness of the main hall. The dragon fireplace was in front of him. There had been a fire earlier in the evening and the burnt-out logs were still smouldering in the hearth. Alex held his hands against the glow, trying to draw a little warmth into himself. Everything was silent. The empty corridors stretched into the distance, illuminated by a few low-watt bulbs that had been left on at intervals. Only now did it occur to Alex that he could have been mistaken from the start. Perhaps the doors were locked every night as part of the security. Perhaps he had jumped too quickly to the wrong conclusion and there was nothing going on after all.

"No...!"

It was a boy's voice. A long, quavering shout that echoed through the school. A moment later, Alex heard feet stamping along a wooden corridor somewhere above. He looked for somewhere to hide and found it inside the fireplace, right next to the logs. The actual fire was contained in a metal basket. There was a wide space on each side between the basket and the brickwork that swept up to become the chimney. Alex crouched low, feeling the heat on the side of his face and legs. He looked out, past the two dragons, waiting to see what would happen.

Three people were coming down the stairs. Mrs Stellenbosch was the first. She was followed by two of the guards, dragging something between them. It was a boy! He was face-down, dressed only in his pyjamas, his bare feet sliding down the stone steps. Mrs Stellenbosch opened the library door and went in. The two guards followed. The door crashed shut. The silence returned.

It had all happened very quickly. Alex had been

unable to see the boy's face. But he was sure he knew who it was. He had known just from the sound of his voice.

James Sprintz.

Alex eased himself out of the fireplace and crossed the hall, making for the library door. There was no sound coming from the other side. He knelt down and looked through the keyhole. No lights were on inside the room. He could see nothing. What should he do? If he went back upstairs, he could make it back to his room without being seen. He could wait until the doors were unlocked and then slip into bed. Nobody would know he had been out.

But the only person in the school who had shown him any kindness was on the other side of the library door. He had been dragged down here. Perhaps he was being brainwashed ... beaten, even. Alex couldn't just turn round and leave him.

Alex had made his decision. He threw open the door and walked in.

The library was empty.

He stood in the doorway, blinking. The library only had one door. All the windows were closed. There was no sign that anyone had been there. The suit of armour stood in its alcove at the end, watching him as he moved forward. Could he have been mistaken? Could Mrs Stellenbosch and the guards have gone into a different room?

Alex went over to the alcove and looked behind the armour, wondering if it might conceal a second exit. There was nothing. He tapped a knuckle against the wall. Curiously, it seemed to be made of metal, but unlike the wall across the stairs there was no handle, nothing to suggest a way through.

There was nothing more he could do here. Alex decided to go back to his room before he was discovered.

But he had only just made it to the first floor when he heard voices once again ... more guards, walking slowly down the corridor. Alex saw a door and slipped inside, once again ducking out of sight. He was in the laundry room. There was a washing-machine, a tumble-drier and two iron-ing-boards. At least it was warm in here. He felt himself surrounded by soap fumes.

The guards had gone. There was a metallic click that seemed to stretch the length of the corridor and Alex realized that all the doors had been unlocked at the same time. He could go back to bed.

He crept out and hurried forward. His footsteps took him past James Sprintz's room, next to his own. He noticed that James's door was open. And then a voice called out from inside.

"Alex?" It was James.

No. That wasn't possible. But there was someone in his room.

Alex looked inside. The light went on.

It *was* James. He was sitting up in bed, bleary-eyed, as if he had just woken up. Alex stared at him. He was wearing the same pyjamas as the boy he had just seen dragged into the library ... but that *couldn't* have been him. It must have been someone else.

"What are you doing?" James asked.

"I thought I heard something," Alex said.

"But you're dressed. And you're soaking wet!" James looked at his watch. "It's almost three..."

Alex was surprised that so much time had passed. It had only been two-fifteen when he'd woken up. "Are you all right?" he asked.

"Yeah."

"You haven't...?"

"What?"

"Nothing. I'll see you later."

Alex crept back to his own room. He closed the door, then stripped off his wet clothes, dried himself with a towel and got back into bed. If it wasn't James he had seen being taken into the library, who was it? And yet it *had* been James. He had heard the cry, seen the limp form on the stairs. So why was James lying now?

Alex closed his eyes and tried to get back to sleep. The movements of the night had created more puzzles and had solved nothing. But at least he'd got something out of it all.

He now knew how to get up to the second floor.

SEEING DOUBLE

James was already eating his breakfast when Alex came down; eggs, bacon, toast and tea. He had the same breakfast every day. He raised a hand in greeting as Alex came in. But the moment he saw him, Alex got the feeling that something was wrong. James was smiling but he seemed somehow distant, as if his thoughts were on other things.

"So what was all that about last night?" James asked.

"I don't know..." Alex was tempted to tell James everything – even the fact that he was here under a false name and had been sent to spy on the school. But he couldn't do it. Not here, so close to the other boys. "I think I had some sort of bad dream."

"Did you go sleepwalking in the snow?"

"No. I thought I saw something, but I couldn't have. I just had a weird night." He changed the subject, lowering his voice. "Have you thought any more about your plan?" he asked.

"What plan?"

"Skiing."

"We're not allowed to ski."

"I mean ... escaping."

James smiled as if he'd only just remembered what Alex was talking about. "Oh – I've changed my mind," he said.

"What d'you mean?"

"If I ran away, my dad would only send me back again. There's no point. I might as well grin and bear it. Anyway, I'd never get all the way down the mountain. The snow's too thin."

Alex stared at James. Everything he was saying was the exact opposite of what he had said the day before. He almost wondered if this was the same boy. But of course it was. He was as untidy as ever. The bruises – fading now – were still there on his face. Dark hair, dark brown eyes, pale skin – it was James. And yet at the same time, something had happened. He was sure of it.

Then James twisted round and Alex saw that Mrs Stellenbosch had come into the room, wearing a particularly nasty lime-green dress that just came down to her knees. "Good morning, boys!" she announced. "We're starting today's lessons in ten minutes. The first lesson is history in the tower room." She walked over to Alex's table. "James, I hope you're going to join us today?"

James shrugged. "All right, Mrs Stellenbosch."

"Excellent. We're looking at the life of Adolf Hitler. Such an interesting man. I'm sure you'll find it most valuable." She walked away.

Alex turned to James. "You're going to lessons?"

"Why not?" James had finished eating. "I'm stuck here and there isn't much else to do. Maybe I should have gone to lessons before. You shouldn't be so negative, Alex." He waved a finger to underline what he was saying. "You're wasting your time."

Alex froze. He had seen that movement before – the way he had waved his finger. Joe Canterbury, the American boy, had done exactly the same thing yesterday.

Puppets dancing on the same string.

What had happened the night before?

Alex watched James leave with the others. He felt he had lost his only friend at Point Blanc and suddenly he wanted to be away from this place, off the mountain and back in the safe world of Brookland School. There might have been a time when he had wanted this adventure. Now he just wanted out of it. Press the button three times on his GPS device and MI6 would come for him. But he couldn't do that until he had something to report.

Alex knew what he had to do. He got up and left the room.

He had seen the way the night before when he was hiding in the fireplace. The chimney bent and twisted its way to the open air – he had been able to see a chink of light from the bottom. Moonlight. The bricks outside the academy might be too smooth to climb, but inside the chimney they were broken and uneven, with plenty of hand and foot-holds. Maybe there would be a fireplace on the second or third floor. But even if there wasn't, the chimney would still lead him to the roof and – assuming there weren't any guards waiting for him there – he might then be able to find a way down.

Alex reached the fireplace with the two stone dragons. He looked at his watch. Nine o'clock. Lessons would continue until lunch and nobody would wonder where he was. The fire had finally gone out, although the ashes were still warm. Would one of the guards come to clean it? He would just have to hope they would leave it until the afternoon. He looked up the chimney. He could see a narrow slit of bright blue. The sky seemed a very long way away and the chimney was narrower than he had thought. What if he got stuck? He forced the thought out of his head, reached for a crack in the brickwork and pulled himself up.

The inside of the chimney smelled of a thousand fires. Soot hung in the air and Alex couldn't breathe without taking it in. He managed to find some purchase for his feet and pushed, sliding himself about one metre up. Now he was wedged inside, forced into a sitting position with his feet against one wall, his back against the other and his legs and bottom hanging in the air. He wouldn't need to use his hands at all. He only had to straighten his legs to push himself up, using the pressure of his feet against the wall to keep himself in place. Push and slide. He had to be careful. Every movement brought more soot trickling down. He could feel it in his hair. He didn't dare look up. If it went into his eyes he would be blinded. Push and slide again, then again. Not too fast. If his feet slipped he would fall all the way back down. He was already a long way above the fireplace. How far had he come? At least one floor ... meaning that he had to be on his way to the second. If he fell from this height he would break both his legs.

The chimney was getting darker and tighter. The light at the top didn't seem to be getting any nearer. Alex found it difficult to manoeuvre himself. He could barely breathe. His entire throat seemed to be coated in soot. He pushed again and this time his knees banged into brickwork, sending a spasm of pain down to his feet. Pinning himself in place, Alex reached up and tried to feel where he was going. There was an L-shaped wall jutting out above his head. His knees had hit the bottom part of it. But his head was behind the upright section. Whatever the obstruction was, it effectively cut the passageway in half, leaving only the narrowest of gaps for Alex's shoulders and body to pass through.

Once again, the nightmare prospect of getting stuck flashed into his mind. Nobody would ever find him. He would suffocate in the dark.

He gasped for breath and swallowed soot. One last try! He pushed again, his arms stretching out over his head. He felt his back slide up the wall, the rough brickwork tearing at his shirt. Then his hands hooked over what he realized must be the top of the L. He pulled himself up and found himself looking into a second fireplace, sharing the main chimney. That was the obstruction he had just climbed round. Alex levered himself over the top and dived clumsily forward. More logs and ashes broke his fall. He had made it to the second floor!

He crawled out of the fireplace. Only a few weeks before, at Brookland, he'd been reading about Victorian chimney-sweeps; how boys as young as six had been forced into virtual slave labour. He'd never thought he would learn how they had felt. He coughed and spat into the palm of his hand. His saliva was black. He wondered what he must look like. He would need to take a shower before he was seen.

He stood up. The second floor was as silent as the ground and the first. Soot trickled out of his hair and for a moment he was blinded. He propped himself against a statue while he wiped his eyes. Then he looked again. He was leaning on a stone dragon, identical to the one on the ground floor. He looked at the fireplace. That too was identical. In fact—

Alex wondered if he hadn't somehow made a terrible mistake. He was standing in a hall that was the same in every detail as the hall on the ground floor. There were the same corridors, the same staircase, the same fireplace – even the same animal heads staring miserably from the walls. It was as if he had climbed in a circle, arriving back where he had begun. He turned round. No. Here was one difference. There was no main door. He could look down on the front courtyard from the window; there was a guard leaning against a wall, smoking a cigarette. This *was* the second floor. But it had been constructed as a perfect replica of the ground.

Alex tiptoed forward, worried that somebody might have heard him climb out of the fireplace. But there was no one around. He followed the corridor as far as the first door. On the ground floor, this would be the library. Gently, a centimetre at a time, he opened the door. It led into a second library – again the spitting image of the first. It had the same tables and chairs, the same suit of armour guarding the same alcove. He ran an eye along one of the shelves. It even had the same books.

But there was one difference – at least, one difference that Alex could see. He felt as if he had strayed into one of those puzzles they sometimes print in comics or magazines. Two identical pictures. But ten deliberate mistakes. Can you spot them? The mistake here was that there was a large television set on a bracket built into the wall. The television was on. Alex found himself looking at an image of yet another library. He was beginning to feel dizzy. What was the library on the television screen? It couldn't be this one because Alex himself was not being shown. So it had to be the library on the ground floor.

Two identical libraries. You could sit in one and watch the other. But why? What was the point?

It took Alex about ten minutes to discover that the entire second floor was a carbon copy of the ground floor, with the same dining-room, living-room and games room. Alex went over to the snooker table and placed a ball in the middle. It rolled into the corner pocket. The room was on the same slant. A television screen showed the games room downstairs. It was the same as the library; one room spying on another.

He retraced his steps and climbed the stairs to the third floor. He wanted to find his own room, but first he went into James's. It was another perfect copy; not just the furniture but the same film posters, the same mobile hanging over the bed, the same Tintin rocket, the photograph.

Even the same clothes strewn over the floor. So these rooms weren't just built to be the same. They were carefully maintained. Whatever happened downstairs, happened upstairs. But did that mean there had been somebody living here, watching every movement that James Sprintz made, doing everything he did? And if so, had somebody else been doing the same for him?

Alex went next door. It was like stepping into his own room. Again there was the same bed, the same furnishings – and the same television. He turned it on. The picture showed his room on the first floor. There was the GPS device, lying on the bed. There were his wet clothes from the night before. Had somebody been watching when he cut through the window and climbed out into the night? Alex felt a jolt of alarm, then forced himself to relax. This room – the copy of his room – was different. Nobody had moved in here yet. He could tell, just by looking around him. The bed hadn't been slept in. And the smaller details hadn't been copied. There was no GPS device in the duplicate room. No wet clothes. He had left the wardrobe door open downstairs. In here it was closed.

The whole thing was like some sort of mind-bending puzzle. Alex forced himself to think it through. Every single boy who arrived at the academy was watched. All his actions were duplicated. If he hung a poster on the wall of his room, an identical poster was hung in an identical room. There would be someone living in this room doing everything that Alex did. He remembered the figure he had glimpsed the day before ... someone wearing what looked like a white mask. Perhaps that person had been about to move in. But all the evidence suggested that for some reason he wasn't here yet.

And that still left the biggest question of all. What was the point? To spy on the boys was one thing. But to copy everything they did?

A door swung shut and he heard voices, two men walking down the corridor outside. Alex crept over to the door and looked out. He just had time to see Dr Grief walk through a door with another man, a short, plump figure in a white coat. They had gone into the laundry room. Alex slipped out of the duplicate bedroom and followed them.

"...you have completed the work. I am grateful to you, Mr Baxter."

"Thank you, Dr Grief."

They had left the door open. Alex crouched down and looked through. Here at last was a section of the third floor that didn't mirror the first.

There were no washing-machines or ironing-boards here. Instead, Alex found himself looking into a room with a row of sinks and through a second set of doors leading into a fully equipped operating theatre at least twice as big as the laundry room on the first floor. At the centre of the room was an operating table. The walls were lined with shelves containing surgical equipment, chemicals and – scattered across the surface – what looked like black and white photographs.

An operating theatre! What was its role in this bizarre, devilish jigsaw puzzle? The two men had walked into it and were talking together, Grief standing with one hand in his pocket. Alex chose his moment, then slipped into the outer room, crouching down beside one of the sinks. From here he could watch and listen as the two of them talked.

"So, I hope you're pleased with the last operation." It was Mr Baxter who was speaking. He had half turned towards the doors and Alex could see a round, flabby face with yellow hair and a thin moustache. Baxter was wearing a bow tie and a checked suit underneath his white coat. Alex had never seen the man before. He was certain of it. And yet at the same time, he thought he knew him. Another puzzle!

"Entirely," Dr Grief replied. "I saw him as soon as the bandages came off. You have done extremely well."

"I always *was* the best. But that's what you paid for." Baxter chuckled. His voice was oily. "And while we're on that subject, maybe we should talk about my final payment?"

"You have already been paid the sum of one million American dollars."

"Yes, Dr Grief." Baxter smiled. "But I was wondering if you might not like to think about a little ... bonus?"

"I thought we had an agreement." Dr Grief turned his head very slowly. The red spectacles homed in on the other man like searchlights.

"We had an agreement for my work, yes. But my silence is another matter. I was thinking of another quarter of a million. Given the size and the scope of your Gemini Project, it's not so much to ask. Then I'll retire to my little house in Spain and you'll never hear from me again."

"I will never hear from you again?"

"I promise."

Dr Grief nodded. "Yes. I think that is a good idea."

His hand came out of his pocket. Alex saw that

it was holding an automatic pistol with a thick silencer protruding from the barrel. Baxter was still smiling as Grief shot him once, through the middle of the forehead. He was thrown off his feet and onto the operating table. He lay still.

Dr Grief lowered the gun. He went over to a telephone, picked it up and dialled a number. There was a pause while his call was answered.

"This is Grief. I have some garbage in the operating theatre that needs to be removed. Could you please inform the disposal team?"

He put down the phone and, glancing one last time at the still figure on the operating table, walked to the other side of the room. Alex saw him press a button. A section of the wall slid open to reveal a lift on the other side. Dr Grief got in. The lift doors closed.

Alex straightened up, too shocked to think straight. He staggered forward and went into the operating theatre. He knew he had to move fast. The disposal team that Dr Grief had called for would be on their way. But he wanted to know what sort of operations took place here. Mr Baxter had presumably been the surgeon. But for what sort of work had he been paid a million dollars?

Trying not to look at the body, Alex looked around. On one shelf was a collection of surgical knives, as horrible as anything he had ever seen, the blades so sharp that he could almost feel their touch just looking at them. There were rolls of gauze, syringes, bottles containing various liquids. But nothing to say why Baxter had been employed. Alex realized it was hopeless. He knew nothing about medicine. This room could have been used for anything from ingrown toenails to full-blown heart surgery.

And then he saw the photographs. He recognized himself, lying on a bed that he thought he knew too. It was Paris! Room thirteen at the Hotel du Monde. He remembered the black and white bedspread, as well as the clothes he had been wearing that night. The clothes had been removed in most of the photographs. Every inch of him had been photographed, sometimes close-up, sometimes wider. In every picture, his eyes were closed. Looking at himself, Alex knew that he had been drugged and remembered how the dinner with Mrs Stellenbosch had ended.

The photographs disgusted him. He had been manipulated by people who thought he was worth nothing at all. From the moment he had met them, he had disliked Dr Grief and his assistant director. Now he felt pure loathing. He still didn't know what they were doing. But they were evil.

They had to be stopped.

He was shaken out of his thoughts by the sound of footsteps coming up the stairs. The disposal team! He looked around him and cursed. He didn't have time to get out and there was nowhere in the room to hide. Then he remembered the lift. He went over to it and urgently stabbed at the button. The footsteps were getting nearer. He heard voices. Then the panels slid open. Alex stepped into a small silver box. There were five buttons: S, R, 1, 2, 3. He pressed R. He had remembered enough French to know that the R must stand for *rez-de-chaussée*, or ground floor. Hopefully, the lift would take him back where he had begun.

The doors slid shut a few seconds before the guards entered the theatre. Alex felt his stomach lurch as he was carried down. The lift slowed. He realized that the doors could open anywhere. He might find himself surrounded by guards – or by the other boys in the school. Well, it was too late now. He had made his choice. He would just have to cope with whatever he found.

But he was lucky. The doors slid open to reveal the library. Alex assumed this was the real library and not another copy. The room was empty. He stepped out of the lift, then turned round. He was facing the alcove. The lift doors formed the alcove wall. They were brilliantly camouflaged, with the suit of armour now sliced exactly in two, one half on each side. As the doors closed automatically, the armour slid back together again, completing the disguise. Despite himself, Alex had to admire the simplicity of it. The entire building was a fantastic box of tricks.

Alex looked at his hands. They were still filthy. He had forgotten that he was completely covered in soot. He crept out of the library, trying not to leave black footprints on the carpet. Then he hurried back to his room. When he got there, he had to remind himself that it was indeed his room and not the copy two floors above. But the GPS receiver was there – and that was what he most needed.

He knew enough. It was time to call for the cavalry. He pressed the button three times, then went to have a shower.

DELAYING TACTICS

It was raining in London, the sort of rain that seems never to stop. The early evening traffic was huddled together, going nowhere. Alan Blunt was standing at the window looking out over the street when there was a knock at the door. He turned away reluctantly, as if the city at its most damp and dismal held some attraction for him. Mrs Jones came in. She was carrying a sheet of paper. As Blunt sat down behind his desk he noticed the words *Most Urgent* printed in red across the top.

"We've heard from Alex," Mrs Jones said.

"Oh yes?"

"Smithers gave him a GPS transmitter with a built-in panic button. Alex sent a signal to us this morning ... at ten twenty-seven hours, his time."

"Meaning?"

"Either he's in trouble or he's found out enough for us to go in. Either way, we have to pull him out."

"I wonder..." Blunt leaned back in his chair, deep in thought. As a young man, he had gained a first class honours degree in mathematics at Cambridge University. Thirty years later, he still saw life as a series of complicated calculations. "Alex has been at Point Blanc for how long?" he asked.

"A week."

"As I recall, he didn't want to go. According to Sir David Friend, his behaviour at Haverstock Hall was, to say the least, anti-social. Did you know that he knocked out Friend's daughter with a stun dart? Apparently he also nearly got her killed in an incident in a railway tunnel."

"He was playing a part," she said. "Exactly what you told him to do."

"Playing it too well, perhaps," Blunt murmured. "Alex may no longer be one hundred per cent reliable."

"He sent the message." Mrs Jones couldn't keep the exasperation out of her voice. "For all we know, he could be in serious trouble. We gave him the device as an alarm signal. To let us know if he needed help. He's used it. We can't just sit back and do nothing."

"I wasn't suggesting that." Alan Blunt looked

curiously at her. "You're not forming some sort of attachment to Alex Rider, are you?" he asked.

Mrs Jones looked away. "Don't be ridiculous."

"You seem worried about him."

"He's fourteen years old, Alan! He's a child, for heaven's sake!"

"You used to have children."

"Yes." Mrs Jones turned to face him again. "Perhaps that does make a difference. But even you must admit that he's special. We don't have another agent like him. A fourteen year old boy! The perfect secret weapon. My feelings about him have nothing to do with it. We can't afford to lose him."

"I just don't want to go blundering into Point Blanc without any firm information," Blunt said. "First of all, this is France we're talking about – and you know what the French are like. If we're seen to be invading their territory they'll kick up one hell of a fuss. Secondly, Grief has got hold of boys from some of the wealthiest families in the world. If we go storming in with the SAS or whatever, the whole thing could blow up into a major international incident."

"You wanted proof that the school was connected to the deaths of Roscoe and Ivanov," Mrs Jones said. "Alex may have it."

"He may have it and he may not. A twenty-four hour delay shouldn't make a great deal of difference."

"Twenty-four hours?"

"We'll put a unit on standby. They can keep an eye on things. If Alex is in trouble, we'll find out soon enough. It could play to our favour if he's managed to stir things up. It's exactly what we want. Force Grief to show us his hand."

"And if Alex contacts us again?"

"Then we'll go in."

"We may be too late."

"For Alex?" Blunt showed no emotion. "I'm sure you don't need to worry about him, Mrs Jones. He can look after himself."

The telephone rang and Blunt answered it. The interview was over. Mrs Jones got up and left to make the arrangements for an SAS unit to fly into Geneva. Blunt was right, of course. Delaying tactics might work in their favour. Clear it with the French. Find out what was going on. And it was only twenty-four hours.

She would just have to hope Alex could survive that long.

Alex found himself eating his breakfast on his own. For the first time, James Sprintz had decided to join the other boys. There they were – the six of them, suddenly the best of friends. Alex looked carefully at the boy who had once been his friend, trying to see what it was that had changed about him. He knew the answer. It was everything and nothing. James was exactly the same and completely different at the same time.

Alex finished his food and got up. James called out to him. "Why don't you come to class this morning, Alex? It's Latin."

Alex shook his head. "Latin's a waste of time."

"Is that what you think?" James couldn't keep the sneer out of his voice and for a moment Alex was startled. For just one second it hadn't been James talking at all. It had been James who had moved his mouth. But it had been Dr Grief speaking the words.

"You enjoy it," Alex said. He hurried out of the room.

Almost twenty-four hours had passed since he had pressed the panic button on his GPS transmitter. Alex wasn't sure what he had been expecting. A fleet of helicopters flying the Union Jack would have been reassuring. But so far nothing had happened. He even wondered if the alarm signal had worked. At the same time, he was annoyed with himself. He had seen Grief shoot the man called Baxter in the operating theatre and he had panicked. He knew that Grief was a killer. He knew that the academy was far more than the finishing school it pretended to be. But he still didn't have all the answers. What exactly was Dr Grief doing? Was he responsible for the deaths of Michael J. Roscoe and Viktor Ivanov? And if so, why?

The fact was, he didn't know enough. And by the time MI6 arrived, Baxter's body would be buried somewhere in the mountains and there would be nothing to prove there was anything wrong. Alex would look like a fool. He could almost imagine Dr Grief telling his side of the story...

"Yes. There is an operating theatre here. It was built years ago. We never use the second and third floors. There is a lift, yes. It was built before we came. We explained to Alex about the armed guards. They're here for his protection. But as you can see, gentlemen, there is nothing unpleasant happening here. The other boys are fine. Baxter? No, I don't know anyone by that name. Obviously Alex has been having bad dreams. I'm amazed that he was sent here to spy on us. I would ask you to take him with you when you leave..."

He had to find out more – and that meant going

back up to the second floor. Or perhaps down. Alex remembered the letters in the secret lift. R for *rez-de-chaussée*. S had to stand for *sous-sol*. The French for basement.

He went over to the Latin classroom and looked in through the half-open door. Dr Grief was out of sight, but Alex could hear his voice.

"Felix qui potuit rerum cognoscere causas..."

There was the sound of scratching; chalk on a blackboard. And there were the six boys, sitting at their desks, listening intently. James was sitting between Hugo and Tom, taking notes. Alex looked at his watch. They would be there for another hour. He was on his own.

He walked back down the corridor and slipped into the library. He had woken up still smelling faintly of soot and had no intention of making his way back up the chimney. Instead he crossed over to the suit of armour. He knew now that the alcove disguised a pair of elevator doors. They could be opened from inside. Presumably there was some sort of control on the outside too.

It took him just a few minutes to find it. There were three buttons built into the breast-plate of the armour. Even close to, the buttons looked like part of the suit – something the medieval knight would have used to strap the thing on. But when Alex pressed the middle button, the armour moved. A moment later, it split in half again and he found himself looking into the waiting lift.

This time he pressed the bottom button. The lift seemed to travel a long way, as if the basement of the building had been built far underground. Finally the doors slid open again. Alex looked out into a curving passageway with tiled walls that reminded him a little of a London tube station. The air was cold down here. The passage was lit by naked bulbs, screwed into the ceiling at intervals.

He looked out, then ducked back. There was a guard at the end of the corridor, sitting at a table reading a newspaper. Would he have heard the lift doors open? Alex leaned forward again. The guard was absorbed in the sports pages. He hadn't moved. Alex slipped out of the lift and crept down the passage, moving away from him. He reached the corner and turned into a second passageway lined with steel doors. There was nobody else in sight.

Where was he? There had to be something down here or there wouldn't be any need for a guard. Alex went over to the nearest of the doors. There was a spy-hole set in the front and he looked through into a bare white cell with two bunk beds, a toilet and a sink. There were two boys in the cell. One he had never seen before, but he recognized the other. It was the red-haired boy called Tom McMorin. But he had seen Tom in Latin just a few minutes ago! What was he doing here?

Alex moved on to the next cell. This one also held two boys. One was a fair-haired, fit-looking boy with blue eyes and freckles. Once again, he recognized the other. It was James Sprintz. Alex examined the door. There were two bolts, but as far as he could see, no key. He drew back the bolts and jerked the door handle down. The door opened. He went in.

James stood up, astonished to see him. "Alex! What are you doing here?"

Alex closed the door. "We haven't got much time," he said. He was speaking in a whisper even though there was little chance of being overheard. "What happened to you?"

"They came for me the night before last," James said. "They dragged me out of bed and into the library. There was some sort of lift—"

"Behind the armour."

"Yes. I didn't know what they were doing. I thought they were going to kill me. But then they threw me in here."

205

"You've been here for two days?"

"Yes."

Alex shook his head. "I saw you having breakfast upstairs fifteen minutes ago."

"They've made duplicates of us." The other boy had spoken for the first time. He had an American accent. "All of us! I don't know how they've done it or why. But that's what they've done." He glanced at the door with anger in his eyes. "I've been here for months. My name's Paul Roscoe."

"Roscoe? Your dad's—"

"Michael Roscoe."

Alex fell silent. He couldn't tell this boy what had happened to his father and he looked away, afraid that Paul would read it in his eyes.

"How did you get down here?" James asked.

"Listen," Alex said. He was speaking rapidly now. "I was sent here by MI6. My name isn't Alex Friend. It's Alex Rider. Everything's going to be OK. They'll send people in and get you all freed."

"You're ... a *spy*?" James was obviously startled.

Alex nodded. "I'm a sort of spy, I suppose," he said.

"You've opened the door. We can get out of here!" Paul Roscoe stood up, ready to move.

"No!" Alex held up his hands. "You've got to wait. There's no way down the mountain. Stay here for now and I'll come back with help. I promise you. It's the only way."

"I can't—"

"You have to. Trust me, Paul. I'm going to have to lock you back in so that nobody will know I've been here. But it won't be for long. I'll come back!"

Alex couldn't wait for any more argument. He went back to the door and opened it.

Mrs Stellenbosch was standing outside.

He only just had time to register the shock of seeing her. He tried to bring up a hand to protect himself, to twist his body into position for a karate kick. But it was already too late. Her arm shot out, the heel of her hand driving into his face. It was like being hit by a brick wall. Alex felt every bone in his body rattle. White light exploded behind his eyes. Then he was out.

HOW TO RULE THE WORLD

"Open your eyes, Alex. Dr Grief wishes to speak to you."

The words came from across an ocean. Alex groaned and tried to lift his head. He was sitting down, his arms pinned behind his back. The whole side of his face felt bruised and swollen and there was the taste of blood in his mouth. He opened his eyes and waited for the room to come into focus. Mrs Stellenbosch was standing in front of him, her fist curled loosely in her other hand. Alex remembered the force of the blow that had knocked him out. His whole head was throbbing and he ran his tongue over his teeth to see if there were any missing. It was fortunate he had rolled with the punch. Otherwise she might have broken his neck.

Dr Grief was sitting in his golden chair, watching Alex with what might have been curiosity or distaste or perhaps a little of both. There was nobody else in the room. It was still snowing outside and there was a small fire burning in the hearth, but the flames weren't as red as Dr Grief's eyes.

"You have put us to a great deal of inconvenience," he said.

Alex straightened his head. He tried to move his hands, but they had been chained together behind the chair.

"Your name is not Alex Friend. You are not the son of Sir David Friend. Your name is Alex Rider and you are employed by the British Secret Service." Dr Grief was simply stating facts. There was no emotion in his voice.

"We have microphones concealed in the cells," Mrs Stellenbosch explained. "Sometimes it is useful for us to hear the conversations between our young guests. Everything you said was overheard by the guard who summoned me."

"You have wasted our time and our money," Dr Grief continued. "For that you will now be punished. It is not a punishment you will survive."

The words were cold and absolute and Alex felt the fear that they triggered. It coursed through his bloodstream, closing in on his heart. He took a deep breath, forcing himself back under control. He had signalled MI6. They would be on their way to Point Blanc. They might appear any minute now. He just had to play for time.

"You can't do anything to me," he said.

Mrs Stellenbosch lashed out and he was thrown backwards as the back of her hand sliced into the side of his head. Only the chair kept him upright. "When you speak to the director, you refer to him as 'Dr Grief'," she said.

Alex looked round again, his eyes watering. "You can't do anything to me, Dr Grief," he said. "I know everything. I know about the Gemini Project. And I've already told London what I know. If you do anything to me, they'll kill you. They're on their way here now."

Dr Grief smiled and in that single moment Alex knew that nothing he said would make any difference to what was about to happen to him. The man was too confident. He was like a poker player who had not only managed to see all the cards but had stolen the four aces for himself.

"It may well be that your friends are on their way," he said. "But I do not think you have told them anything. We have been through your luggage and found the transmitting device concealed in the GPS receiver. I noted also that it can send out a signal but not a message. Quite how you have learned about the Gemini Project is of no interest to me. I assume you overheard the name whilst eavesdropping at a door. We should have been more careful – but for British intelligence to send in a child ... that was something we could not expect.

"Let us assume then that your friends do come calling. They will find nothing wrong. You yourself will have disappeared. I shall tell them that you ran away. I will say that my men are looking for you even now, but I very much fear you will have died a cold and lingering death on the mountainside. Nobody will guess what I have done here. The Gemini Project will succeed. It has *already* succeeded. And even if your friends do take it upon themselves to kill me, that will make no difference. I cannot be killed, Alex. The world is already mine."

"You mean it belongs to the kids you've hired to act as doubles," Alex said.

"Hired?" Dr Grief muttered a few words to Mrs Stellenbosch in a harsh, guttural language. Alex assumed it must be Afrikaans. Her thick lips parted and she laughed, showing heavy, discoloured teeth. "Is that what you think?" Dr Grief asked. "Is that what you believe?"

"I've seen them."

"You don't know what you've seen. You have no understanding of my genius! Your little mind couldn't begin to encompass what I have achieved." Dr Grief was breathing heavily. He seemed to come to a decision. "It is rare enough for me to come face to face with the enemy," he said. "It has always been my frustration that I will never be able to communicate to the world the brilliance of what I have done. Well, since I have you here – a captive audience, so to speak – I shall allow myself the luxury of describing the Gemini Project. And when you go, screaming, to your death, you will understand that there was never any hope for you. That you could not hope to come up against a man like me and win. Perhaps that will make it easier for you."

"I will smoke, if you don't mind, Doctor," Mrs Stellenbosch said. She took out her cigars and lit one. Smoke danced in front of her eyes.

"I am, as I am sure you are aware, South African," Dr Grief began. "The animals in the hall and in this room are all souvenirs of my time there; shot on safari. I still miss my country. It is the most beautiful place on this planet.

"What you may not know, however, is that for many years I was one of South Africa's foremost

biochemists. I was head of the biology department at the University of Johannesburg. I later
ran the Cyclops Institute for Genetic Research in
Pretoria. But the height of my career came in the
1960s when, although I was still in my twenties,
John Vorster, the prime minister of South Africa,
appointed me Minister for Science—"

"You've already said you're going to kill me,"
Alex said, "but I didn't think that meant you were
going to bore me to death."

Mrs Stellenbosch coughed on her cigar and
advanced on Alex, her fist clenched. But Dr Grief
stopped her. "Let the boy have his little joke," he
said. "There will be pain enough for him later."

The assistant director glowered at Alex.

Dr Grief went on. "I am telling you this, Alex,
only because it will help you understand. You perhaps know nothing about South Africa. English
schoolchildren are, I have found, the laziest and
most ignorant in the world. All that will soon
change! But let me tell you a little bit about my
country, as it was when I was young.

"The white people of South Africa ruled everything. Under the laws that came to be known to
the world as apartheid, black people were not
allowed to live near white people. They could not
marry white people. They could not share white

toilets, restaurants, sports halls or bars. They had to carry passes. They were treated like animals."

"It was disgusting," Alex said.

"It was wonderful!" Mrs Stellenbosch murmured.

"It was indeed perfect," Dr Grief agreed. "But as the years passed, I became aware that it would also be short-lived. The uprising at Soweto, the growing resistance and the way the entire world – including your own, stinking country – ganged up on us, I knew that white South Africa was doomed and I even foresaw the day when power would be handed over to a man like Nelson Mandela."

"A criminal!" Mrs Stellenbosch added. Smoke was dribbling out of her nostrils.

Alex said nothing. It was clear enough that both Dr Grief and his assistant were mad. Just how mad they were was becoming clearer with every word they spoke.

"I looked at the world," Dr Grief said, "and I began to see just how weak and pathetic it was becoming. How could it happen that a country like mine could be given away to people who would have no idea how to run it? And why was the rest of the world so determined for it to be so? I looked around me and I saw that the people of America and Europe had become stupid and weak. The fall of the Berlin Wall only made things worse. I had always admired the Russians, but they quickly became infected with the same disease. And I thought to myself, if I ruled the world, how much stronger it would be. How much better—"

"For you, perhaps, Dr Grief," Alex said. "But not for anyone else."

Grief ignored him. His eyes, behind the red glasses, were brilliant. "It has been the dream of very few men to rule the entire world," he said. "Hitler was one. Napoleon another. Stalin, perhaps, a third. Great men! Remarkable men! But to rule the world in the twenty-first century requires something more than military strength. The world is a more complicated place now. Where does real power lie? In politics. Prime ministers and presidents. But you will also find power in industry, in science, in the media, in oil, in the Internet... Modern life is a great tapestry and if you wish to take control of it all, you must seize hold of every strand.

"This is what I decided to do, Alex. And it was because of my unique position in the unique place that was South Africa that I was able to attempt it." Grief took a deep breath. "What do you know about nuclear transplantation?" he asked.

"I don't know anything," Alex said. "But as you said, I'm an English schoolboy. Lazy and ignorant."

"There is another word for it. Have you heard of cloning?"

Alex almost burst out laughing. "You mean ... like Dolly the sheep?"

"To you it may be a joke, Alex. Something out of science fiction. But scientists have been searching for a way to create exact replicas of themselves for more than a hundred years. The word itself is Greek for 'twig'. Think how a twig starts as one branch but then splits into two. This is exactly what has been achieved with lizards, with sea urchins, with tadpoles and frogs, with mice and, yes, on 5 July 1996, with a sheep. The theory is simple enough. Nuclear transplantation. To take the nucleus out of an egg and replace it with a cell taken from an adult. I won't tire you with the details, Alex. But it is not a joke. Dolly was the perfect copy of a sheep that had died six years before Dolly was born. She was the end result of no less than one hundred years of experimentation. And in all that time, the scientists shared a single dream. To clone an adult human. I have achieved that dream!"

He paused.

"If you want a round of applause, you'll have to take off the handcuffs," Alex said.

"I don't want applause," Grief snarled. "Not from you. What I want from you is your life ... and that I will take."

"So who did you clone?" Alex asked. "Not Mrs Stellenbosch, I hope. I'd have thought one of her was more than enough."

"Who do you *think*? I cloned myself!" Dr Grief grabbed hold of the arms of his chair, a king on the throne of his own imagination. "Twenty years ago I began my work," he explained. "I told you – I was Minister for Science. I had all the equipment and money that I needed. Also – this was South Africa! The rules that hampered other scientists around the world did not apply to me. I was able to use human beings – political prisoners – for my experiments. Everything was done in secret. I worked without stopping for twenty years. And then, when I was ready, I stole a very large amount of money from the South African government and moved here.

"It took me another six years before I was ready but then, after countless experiments, working day and night, I did it! I cloned myself ... and not just once. Sixteen times. Do you have any idea what an acheivement that was, Alex?"

"It was genius," Mrs Stellenbosch muttered.

"It would be another whole decade before an English scientist would astonish the world by cloning a sheep."

"Baaah!" Mrs Stellenbocsh exclaimed.

"But I had done it already here, at Point Blanc. Sixteen exact copies of me. With my looks. My brains. My ambition. And my determination."

"Were they all as mad as you too?" Alex asked, and flinched as Mrs Stellenbosch hit him again, this time in the stomach. But he wanted to make them angry. If they were angry, they might make mistakes.

"To begin with they were babies," Dr Grief said. "Sixteen babies from sixteen mothers – who were themselves biologically irrelevant. They would grow up to become replicas of myself. I have had to wait fourteen years for the babies to become boys and the boys to become teenagers. Eva here has looked after all of them. You have met them – some of them."

"Tom, Cassian, Nicolas, Hugo, Joe. And James..." Now Alex understood why they had somehow all looked the same.

"Do you see, Alex? Do you have any idea what I have done? I will never die because even when this body is finished with, I will live on in them. I am them and they are me. We are one and the same."

He smiled again. "I was helped in all this by Eva Stellenbosch, who had also worked with me in the South African government. She had worked in the SASS – our own secret service. She was one of their principal interrogators."

"Happy days!" Mrs Stellenbosch smiled.

"Together we set up the academy. Because, you see, that was the second part of my plan. I was creating sixteen copies of myself. But that wasn't enough. You remember what I said about the strands of the tapestry? I had to bring them here, to draw them together—"

"To replace them with copies of yourself!" Suddenly Alex saw it all. It was totally insane. But it was the only way to make sense of everything he had seen.

Dr Grief nodded. "It was my observation that families with wealth and power frequently had children who were ... troubled. Parents with no time for their sons. Sons with no love for their parents. These children became my targets, Alex. Because, you see, I wanted what these children had.

"Take a boy like Hugo Vries. One day his father will leave him with a fifty per cent stake in the world's diamond market. Or Tom McMorin; his mother has newspapers all over the world. Or Joe Canterbury; his father at the Pentagon, his mother a senator. What better start for a life in politics? What better start for a future president of the United States, even? Fifteen of the most promising children who have been sent here to Point Blanc, I have replaced with copies of myself. Surgically altered, of course, to look exactly like the originals."

"Baxter, the man you shot—"

"You have been busy, Alex." For the first time, Dr Grief looked surprised. "The late Mr Baxter was a plastic surgeon. I found him working in Harley Street, London. He had gambling debts. It was easy to bring him under my control and it was his job to operate on my family, to change their faces, their skin colour – and where necessary their bodies – so that they would exactly resemble the teenagers they replaced. From the moment the real teenagers arrived here at Point Blanc, they were kept under observation—"

"With identical rooms on the second and third floors."

"Yes. My doubles were able to watch their targets on television monitors. To copy their every movement. To learn their mannerisms. To eat like them. To speak like them. In short, to become them."

"It would never have worked!" Alex twisted in his chair, trying to find some leverage in the handcuffs. But the metal was too tight. He couldn't move. "Parents would know that the children you sent back were fakes!" he insisted. "Any mother would know it wasn't her son, even if he looked the same."

Mrs Stellenbosch giggled. She had finished her cigar. Now she lit another.

"You are quite wrong, Alex," Dr Grief said. "In the first place, you are talking about busy, hard-working parents who had little or no time for their children in the first place. And you forget that the very reason why these people sent their sons here was because they *wanted* them to change. It is the reason why all parents send their sons to private schools. Oh yes – they think the schools will make their children better, more clever, more confident. They would actually be disappointed if those children came back the same.

"And nature, too, is on our side. A boy of fourteen leaves home for six or seven weeks. By the time he gets back, nature will have made its mark. The boy will be taller. He will be fatter or thinner. Even his voice will have changed. It's all part of puberty and the parents when they see him will say, 'Oh Tom, you've got so big – and you're so grown up!' And they will suspect nothing. In fact, they would be worried if the boy had *not* changed."

"But Roscoe guessed, didn't he?" Alex knew he had arrived at the truth, the reason why he had been sent here in the first place. He knew why Roscoe and Ivanov had died.

"There have been two occasions when the parents did not believe what they saw," Dr Grief admitted. "Michael J. Roscoe in New York. And General Viktor Ivanov in Moscow. Neither man completely guessed what had happened. But they were unhappy. They argued with their sons. They asked too many questions."

"And the sons told you what had happened."

"You might say that I told myself. The sons, after all, are me. But yes. Michael Roscoe knew something was wrong and called MI6 in London. I presume that is how you were unlucky enough to become involved. I had to pay to have Roscoe killed just as I paid for the death of Ivanov. But it was to be expected that there would be problems. Two out of sixteen is not so catastrophic, and of course it makes no difference to my plans. In many ways, it even helps me. Michael J. Roscoe left his entire fortune to his son. And I understand that the Russian president is taking a personal interest in Dimitry Ivanov following the loss of his father.

"In short, the Gemini Project has been an outstanding success. In a few days' time, the last of the children will leave Point Blanc to take their places in the heart of their families. Once I am satisfied that they have all been accepted, I will, I fear, have to dispose of the originals. They will die painlessly.

"The same cannot be said for you, Alex Rider. You have caused me a great deal of annoyance. I propose, therefore, to make an example of you." Dr Grief reached into his pocket and took out a device that looked like an old-fashioned pager. It had a single button, which he pressed. "What is the first lesson tomorrow morning, Eva?" he asked.

"Double biology," Mrs Stellenbosch replied.

"As I thought. You have perhaps been to biology lessons where a frog or a rat has been dissected, Alex," he said. "For some time now, my children have been asking to see a human dissection. This is no surprise to me. At the age of fourteen, I first attended a human dissection myself. Tomorrow morning, at nine-thirty, their wish will be granted. You will be brought into the laboratory and we will open you up and have a look at you. We will not be using anaesthetic and it will be interesting to see how long you survive before your heart gives out. And then, of course, we shall dissect your heart."

"You're sick!" Alex yelled. Now he was thrashing about in the chair, trying to break the wood, trying to get the handcuffs to come apart. But it was hopeless. The metal cut into him. The chair rocked but stayed in one piece. "You're a madman!"

"I am a scientist!" Dr Grief spat the words. "And that is why I am giving you a scientific death. At least in your last minutes you will have been some use to me." He looked past Alex. "Take him away and search him thoroughly. Then lock him up for the night. I'll see him again first thing tomorrow morning."

Alex had seen Dr Grief summon the guards but he hadn't heard them come in. He was seized from behind, the handcuffs were unlocked and he was jerked backwards out of the room. His last sight of Dr Grief was of the man stretching out his hands to warm them at the fire, the twisting flames reflected in his glasses. Mrs Stellenbosch smiled and blew out smoke.

Then the door slammed shut and Alex was dragged down the corridor knowing that Blunt and the secret service had to be on their way – but wondering if they would arrive before it was too late.

BLACK RUN

The cell measured two metres by four metres and contained a bunk bed with no mattress and a chair. The door was solid steel. Alex had heard a key turn in the lock after it was closed. He had not been given anything to eat or drink. The cell was cold but there were no blankets on the bed.

At least the guards had left the handcuffs off. They had searched Alex expertly, removing everything they had found in his pockets. They had also removed his belt and the laces of his shoes. Perhaps Dr Grief had thought he would hang himself. He needed Alex fresh and alive for the biology lesson.

It was about two o'clock in the morning but Alex hadn't slept. He had tried to put out of his mind everything Grief had told him. That wasn't important now. He knew that he had to escape before nine-thirty because – like it or not – it seemed he was on his own. More than thirty-six hours had passed since he had pressed the panic button that Smithers had given him – and nothing had happened. Either the machine hadn't worked or for some reason MI6 had decided not to come. Of course it was possible that something might happen before breakfast the next day. But Alex wasn't prepared to risk it. He had to get out. Tonight.

For the twentieth time he went over to the door and knelt down, listening carefully. The guards had dragged him back down to the basement. He was in a corridor separate from the other prisoners. Although everything had happened very quickly, Alex had tried to remember where he was being taken. Out of the lift and turn left. Round the corner and then down a second passageway to a door at the end. He was on his own. And listening through the door, he was fairly sure that they hadn't posted a guard outside.

It had to be now – the middle of the night. When they had searched him, the guards hadn't quite taken everything. Neither of them had even noticed the gold stud in his ear. What had

Smithers said? "It's a small but very powerful explosive. Separating the two pieces activates it. Count to ten and it'll blow a hole in just about anything..."

Now was the time to put it to the test.

Alex reached up and unscrewed the ear-stud. He pulled it out of his ear, slipped the two pieces into the keyhole of the door, stepped back and counted to ten.

Nothing happened. Was the stud broken, like the GPS transmitter? Alex was about to give up when there was a sudden flash, an intense sheet of orange flame. Fortunately there was no noise. The flare continued for about five seconds, then went out. Alex went back to the door. The stud had burned a hole in it, the size of a two pound coin. The melted metal was still glowing. Alex reached out and pushed. The door swung open.

Alex felt a momentary surge of excitement, but he forced himself to remain calm. He might be out of the cell but he was still in the basement of the academy. There were guards everywhere. He was on top of a mountain with no skis and no obvious way down. He wasn't safe yet. Not by a long way.

He slipped out of the room and followed the corridor back round to the lift. He was tempted to find the other boys and release them but he knew that they couldn't help. Taking them out of their cells would only put them in danger. Somehow, he found his way back to the lift. He noticed that the guard-post he had seen that morning was empty. Either the man had gone to make himself a coffee or Grief had relaxed security in the academy. With Alex and all the other boys locked up, there was nobody left to guard. Or so they thought. Alex hurried forward. It seemed that luck was on his side.

He took the lift back to the first floor. He knew that his only way off the mountain lay in his bedroom. Grief would certainly have examined everything he had brought with him. But what would he have done with it? Alex crept down the dimly lit corridor and into his room. And there it all was, lying in a heap on his bed. The ski suit. The goggles. Even the remaining plastic packets of hand warmers. Alex heaved a sigh of relief. He was going to need all of it.

He had already worked out what he was going to do. He couldn't ski off the mountain. He still had no idea where the skis were kept. But there was more than one way to take to the snow. Alex froze as a guard walked along the corridor outside the room. So not everyone at the academy was asleep! He would have to move fast. As soon as the broken cell door was discovered, the alarm would be raised.

He waited until the guard had gone, then stole into the laundry room a few doors down. When he came out, he was carrying a long flat object made of lightweight aluminium. He carried it into his bedroom, closed the door and turned on one small lamp. He was afraid that the guard would see the light if he returned. But he couldn't work in the dark. It was a risk he had to take.

He had stolen an ironing-board.

Alex had only been snowboarding three times in his life. The first time, he had spent most of the day falling or sitting on his bottom. Snowboarding is a lot harder to learn than skiing – but as soon as you get the hang of it, you can advance fast. By the third day, Alex had learned how to ride, edging and cutting his way down the beginner slopes. He needed a snowboard now. The ironing-board would have to do.

He picked up the two of the hand warmers and tore them open. Quickly, he manipulated the grey putty and pressed it underneath the metal surface. He hoped he'd got it right. The ironing-board was wider than he would have liked. He knew that the longer the board, the faster he could go, but if he left it too long he would have no control. The ironing-board was flat. Without any curve at the front – or nose as it was called – he would be at the mercy of every bump or upturned root. But there was nothing he could do. There was a hiss and once again smoke rose into the air as the putty ate into the metal, cutting it into the shape Alex wanted. About half the ironing-board fell away. Being careful not to burn his hands on the still smouldering edges, Alex levered up the other half. It almost reached his chest, with a point at one end and a curve at the back. Perfect.

He used more of the putty to burn off the supports, leaving about six centimetres sticking up. He knew that the rider and the board can only work together if the bindings are right and he had nothing; no boots, no straps, no highback to support his heel. He was just going to have to improvize. While the metal cooled, he tore two strips of sheet from the bed, then slipped into his ski suit. He would have to tie one of his trainers to what was left of the ironing-board supports. It was horribly dangerous. If he fell, he would dislocate his foot.

But he was almost ready. Quickly Alex zipped up the ski suit. Smithers had said it was bullet-proof and it occurred to him that he was probably going to need it. He put the goggles around his neck. The window still hadn't been repaired. He dropped the ironing-board out, then climbed out after it.

There was no moon now. Alex found the switch concealed in the goggles and turned it. He heard a soft hum as the hidden battery activated, and suddenly the side of the mountain glowed an eerie green and Alex was able to see the trees and the deserted ski-run falling away.

He carried the ironing-board over to the edge of the snow and used the sheet to tie it to his foot. Carefully he took up his position, his right foot at forty degrees, his left foot at twenty. He was goofy-footed. That was what the instructor had told him. His feet should have been the other way round. But this was no time to worry about technique. Alex stood where he was, contemplating what he was about to do. He had only ever done green and blue runs – the colours given to the beginner and intermediate slopes. He knew from James that this mountain was an expert black all the way down. His breath rose up in green clouds in front of his eyes. Could he do it? Could he trust himself?

An alarm bell exploded behind him. Lights came on throughout the academy. Alex pushed forward and set off, picking up speed with every second. The decision had been made for him. Now, whatever happened, there could be no going back.

Dr Grief, wearing a long silver dressing-gown, stood beside the open window in Alex's room. Mrs Stellenbosch was also in a robe – hers was pink silk and looked strangely hideous, hanging off her lumpy body. Three guards stood watching them, waiting for instructions.

"Who searched the boy?" Dr Grief asked. He had already been shown the cell door with the circular hole burnt into the lock.

None of the guards answered, but their faces had gone pale.

"This is a question to be answered in the morning," Dr Grief continued. "For now, all that matters is that we find him and kill him."

"He must be walking down the mountainside!" Mrs Stellenbosch said. "He has no skis. He won't make it. We can wait until morning and pick him up in the helicopter."

"I think the boy may be more inventive than we believe." Dr Grief picked up the remains of the ironing-board. "You see? He has improvized some sort of sleigh or toboggan. All right..." He had

233

come to a decision. Mrs Stellenbosch was glad to see the certainty return to his eyes. "I want two men on snowmobiles, following him down. Now!" One of the guards hurried out of the room.

"What about the unit at the foot of the mountain?" Mrs Stellenbosch said.

"Indeed." Dr Grief smiled. He had always kept a guard and a driver at the end of the last valley in case anybody ever tried to leave the academy on skis. It was a precaution that was about to pay off. "Alex Rider will have to arrive in la Vallée de Fer. Whatever he's using to get down, he'll be unable to cross the railway line. We can have a machine-gun set up waiting for him. Assuming he does manage to get that far, he'll be a sitting duck."

"Excellent," Mrs Stellenbosch purred.

"I would have liked to watch him die. But, yes. The Rider boy has no hope at all. And we can return to bed."

Alex was on the edge of space, seemingly falling to certain death. In snowboarding language, he was catching air – meaning that he had shot away from the ground. Every ten metres he went forward, the mountainside disappeared another five metres downward. He felt the world spin around him. The wind whipped into his face. Then some-how he brought himself in line with the next section of the slope and shot down, steering the ironing-board ever further from Point Blanc. He was moving at a terrifying speed, trees and rock formations passing in a luminous green blur across his night-vision goggles. In some ways the steeper slopes made it easier. At one point he had tried to make a landing on a flat part of the mountain – a tabletop – to slow himself down. He had hit the ground with such a bone-shattering crash that he had nearly blacked out and had taken the next twenty metres almost totally blind.

The ironing-board was shuddering and shaking crazily and it took all his strength to make the turns. He was trying to follow the natural fall-line of the mountain but there were too many obstacles in the way. What he most dreaded was melted snow. If the board landed on a patch of mud at this speed, he would be thrown and killed. And he knew that the further down he went, the greater the danger would become.

But he had been travelling for five minutes and so far he had only fallen twice – both times into thick banks of snow that had protected him. How far down could it be? He tried to remember what James Sprintz had told him, but thinking was impossible at this speed. He was having to use every ounce of his conscious thought simply to stay upright.

He reached a small lip where the surface was level and drove the edge of the board into the snow, bringing himself to a skidding halt. Ahead of him the ground fell away alarmingly. He hardly dared look down. There were thick clumps of trees to the left and to the right. In the distance there was just a green blur. The goggles could only see so far.

And then he heard the noise coming up behind him. The scream of at least two – maybe more – engines. Alex looked back over his shoulder. For a moment there was nothing. But then he saw them – black flies swimming into his field of vision. There were two of them, heading his way.

Grief's men were riding specially adapted Yamaha Mountain Max snowmobiles equipped with 700cc triple-cylinder engines. The bikes were flying over the snow on their 141-inch tracks, effortlessly moving five times faster than Alex. The 300-watt headlights had already picked him out. Now the men sped towards him, cutting the distance between them with every second that passed.

Alex leapt forward, diving into the next slope. At the same moment, there was a sudden chatter, a series of distant cracks, and the snow leapt up all around him. Grief's men had machine-guns built into their snowmobiles! Alex yelled as he swooped down the mountainside, barely able to control the sheet of metal under his feet. The makeshift binding was tearing at his ankle. The whole thing was vibrating crazily. He couldn't see. He could only keep going, trying to keep his balance, hoping that the way ahead was clear.

The headlights of the nearest Yamaha shot out and Alex saw his own shadow stretching ahead of him on the snow. There was another chatter from the machine-gun and Alex ducked down, almost feeling the fan of bullets spray over his head. The second bike screamed up, coming parallel with him. He *had* to get off the mountainside. Otherwise he would be shot or run over. Or both.

He forced the board onto its edge, making a turn. He had seen a gap in the trees and he made for it. Now he was racing through the forest, with branches and trunks whipping past like crazy animations in a computer game. Could the snowmobiles follow him through here? The question was answered by another burst from the machine-guns, ripping through the leaves and branches.

Alex searched for a narrower path. The board shuddered and he was almost thrown forward head first. The snow was getting thinner! He edged and turned, heading for two of the thickest trees. He passed between them with millimetres to spare. Now – follow that!

The Yamaha snowmobile had no choice. The rider had run out of paths. He was travelling too fast to stop. He tried to follow Alex between the trees, but the snowmobile was too wide. Alex heard the collision. There was a terrible crunch, then a scream, then an explosion. A ball of orange flame leapt over the trees, sending black shadows in a crazy dance. Ahead of him Alex saw another hillock and, beyond it, a gap in the trees. It was time to leave the forest.

He swooped up the hillock and out, once again catching air. As he left the trees behind him, two metres above the ground, he saw the second snowmobile. It had caught up with him. For a moment the two of them were side by side. Alex doubled forward and grabbed the nose of his board. Still in mid-air, he twisted the tip of the board, bringing the tail swinging round. He had timed it perfectly. The tail slammed into the second rider's head, almost throwing him out of his seat. The rider yelled and lost control. His snowmobile jerked sideways as if trying to make an impossibly tight turn. Then it left the ground, cartwheeling over and over again. The rider was thrown off, then screamed as the snowmobile completed its final turn and landed on top of him. Man and machine were bounced across the surface of the snow and then lay still. Alex slammed into the snow and skidded to halt, his breath clouding green in front of his eyes.

A second later he pushed off again. Ahead of him he could see that all the pistes were leading into a single valley. This must be the bottleneck called la Vallée de Fer. So he'd actually done it! He'd reached the bottom of the mountain. But now he was trapped. There was no other way round. He could see lights in the distance. A city. Safety. But he could also see the railway line stretching right across the valley, from left to right, protected on both sides by an embankment and a barbed wire fence. The glow from the city illuminated everything. On one side the track came out of the mouth of a tunnel. It ran for about a hundred metres in a straight line before a sharp bend carried it round the other side of the valley and it disappeared from sight.

The two men in the grey van saw Alex

snowboarding towards them. They were parked on a road on the other side of the railway line and had been waiting for only a few minutes. They hadn't seen the explosion and wondered what had happened to the two guards on their snowmobiles. But that wasn't their concern. Their orders were to kill the boy. And there he was, right out in the open, expertly managing the last black run through the valley. Every second brought him closer to them. There was nowhere for him to hide. The machine-gun was a Belgian FN MAG and would cut him in half.

Alex saw the van. He saw the machine-gun aiming at him. He couldn't stop. It was too late to change direction. He had come this far, but now he was finished. He felt the strength draining out of him. Where were MI6? Why did he have to die, out here, on his own?

And then there was a sudden blast as a train thundered out of the tunnel. It was a goods train, travelling at about twenty miles an hour. It had at least thirty carriages, pulled by a diesel engine, and it formed a moving wall between Alex and the gun, protecting him. But it would only be there for a few seconds. He had to move fast.

Barely knowing what he was doing, Alex found

a last mound of snow and, using it as a launch pad, swept up into the air. Now he was level with the train ... now above it. He shifted his weight and came down onto the roof of one of the carriages. The surface was covered in ice and for a moment he thought he would fall off the other side, but he managed to swing round so that he was snowboarding along the carriage tops, jumping from one to another, at the same time being swept along the track – away from the gun – in a blast of freezing air.

He had done it! He had got away! He was still sliding forward, the train adding its speed to his own. No snowboarder had ever moved so fast. But then the train reached the bend in the track. The board had no purchase on the icy surface. As the train sped round to the left, the centrifugal force threw Alex to the right. Once again he soared into the air. But he had finally run out of snow.

Alex hit the ground like a rag doll. The snowboard was torn off his feet. He bounced twice, then hit a wire fence and came to rest with blood spreading around a deep gash in his head. His eyes were closed.

The train ploughed on through the night.

Alex lay still.

AFTER THE FUNERAL

The ambulance raced down the Avenue Maquis de Gresivaudan in the north of Grenoble, heading towards the river. It was five o'clock in the morning and there was no traffic yet, no need for the siren. Just before the river it turned off into a compound of ugly modern buildings. This was the second biggest hospital in the city. The ambulance pulled up outside the *Service des Urgences*. Paramedics ran towards it as the back doors flew open.

Mrs Jones got out of her hired car and watched as the limp, unmoving body was lowered on a stretcher, transferred to a trolley and rushed in through the double doors. There was already a saline drip attached to his arm. An oxygen mask covered his face. It had been snowing up in the mountains but down here there was only a dull drizzle, sweeping across the pavements. A doctor in a white coat was bending over the stretcher. He sighed and shook his head. Mrs Jones saw this. She crossed the road and followed the stretcher in.

A thin man with close-cropped hair, wearing a black jersey and padded waistcoat, had also been watching the hospital. He saw Mrs Jones without knowing who she was. He had also seen Alex. He took out a mobile telephone and made a call. Dr Grief would want to know...

Three hours later the sun had risen over the city. Grenoble is largely modern and even with its perfect mountain setting it struggles to be attractive. On this damp, cloudy day it was clearly failing.

Outside the hospital, a car drew up and Eva Stellenbosch got out. She was wearing a silver and white chessboard suit, with a hat perched on her ginger hair. She carried a leather handbag and for once she had put on make-up. She wanted to look elegant. She looked like a man in drag.

She walked into the hospital and found the main reception desk. There was a young nurse sitting behind a bank of telephones and computer screens. Mrs Stellenbosch addressed her in fluent French.

"Excuse me," she said. "I understand that a young boy was brought here this morning. His name is Alex Friend."

"One moment, please." The nurse entered the name into her computer. She read the information on the screen and her face became serious. "May I ask who you are?"

"I am the assistant director of the academy at Point Blanc. He is one of our students."

"Are you aware of the extent of his injuries, madame?"

"I was told that he was involved in a snowboarding accident." Mrs Stellenbosch took out a small handkerchief and dabbed at her eyes.

"He tried to snowboard down the mountains at night. He was involved in a collision with a train. His injuries are very serious, madame. The doctors are operating on him now."

Mrs Stellenbosch nodded, swallowing her tears. "My name is Eva Stellenbosch," she said. "May I wait for any news?"

"Of course, madame."

Mrs Stellenbosch took a seat in the reception area. For the next hour she watched as people came and went, some walking, some in wheelchairs. There were other people waiting for news of other patients. One of them, she noticed, was a serious-looking woman with black hair, badly cut, and very black eyes. She was from England – glancing occasionally at a copy of the London *Times*.

Then a door opened and a doctor came out. Doctors have a certain face when they come to give bad news. This doctor had it now. "Madame Stellenbosch?" he asked.

"Yes?"

"You are the director of the school...?"

"The assistant director, yes."

The doctor sat next to her. "I am very sorry, madame. Alex Friend died a few minutes ago." He waited while she absorbed the news. "He had multiple fractures. His arms, his collar-bone, his leg. He had also fractured his skull. We operated, but unfortunately there had been massive internal bleeding. He went into shock and we were unable to bring him round."

Mrs Stellenbosch nodded, struggling for words. "I must notify his family," she whispered.

"Is he from this country?"

"No. He is English. His father ... Sir David Friend ... I'll have to tell him." Mrs Stellenbosch got to her feet. "Thank you, doctor. I'm sure you did everything you could."

Out of the corner of her eye, Mrs Stellenbosch

noticed that the woman with the black hair had also stood up, letting her newspaper fall to the floor. She had overheard the conversation. She was looking shocked.

Both women left the hospital at the same time. Neither of them spoke.

The aircraft waiting on the runway was a Lockheed Martin C-130 Hercules. It had landed just after midday. Now it waited beneath the clouds while three vehicles drove towards it. One was a police car, one a Jeep and one an ambulance.

The Saint-Geoirs airport at Grenoble does not see many international flights, but the plane had flown out from England that morning. From the other side of the perimeter fence, Mrs Stellenbosch watched through a pair of high-powered binoculars. A small military escort had been formed. Four men in French uniforms. They had lifted up a coffin which seemed pathetically small when balanced on their broad shoulders. The coffin was simple. Pinewood with silver handles. A Union Jack was folded in a square in the middle.

Marching in time, they carried the coffin towards the waiting plane. Mrs Stellenbosch focused the binoculars and saw the woman from the hospital. She had been travelling in the police car. She stood watching as the coffin was loaded into the plane, then got back into the car and was driven away. By now, Mrs Stellenbosch knew who she was. Dr Grief kept extensive files and had quickly identified her as Mrs Jones; deputy to Alan Blunt, head of Special Operations for MI6.

Mrs Stellenbosch stayed until the end. The doors of the plane were closed. The Jeep and the ambulance left. The plane's propellers began to turn and it lumbered forward onto the runway. A few minutes later it took off. As it thundered into the air, the clouds opened as if to receive it and for a moment its silver wings were bathed in brilliant sunlight. Then the clouds rolled back and the plane disappeared.

Mrs Stellenbosch took out her mobile. She dialled a number and waited until she was connected. "The little swine has gone," she said.

She got back into her car and drove away.

After Mrs Jones had left the airport, she returned to the hospital and took the stairs to the second floor. She came to a pair of doors guarded by a policeman who nodded and let her pass through. On the other side was a corridor leading to a private wing. She walked down to a door, this one also guarded. She didn't knock. She went straight in.

Alex Rider was standing by the window, looking out at the view of Grenoble on the other side of the River Isère. Outside, high above him, five steel and glass bubbles moved slowly along a cable, ferrying tourists up to the Fort de la Bastille. He turned round as Mrs Jones came in. There was a bandage around his head but otherwise he seemed unhurt.

"You're lucky to be alive," she said.

"I thought I was dead," Alex replied.

"Let's hope Dr Grief believes as much." Despite herself, Mrs Jones couldn't keep the worry out of her eyes. "It really was a miracle," she said. "You should have at least broken something."

"The ski suit protected me," Alex said. He tried to think back to the whirling, desperate moment when he had been thrown off the train. "There was undergrowth. And the fence sort of caught me." He rubbed his leg and winced. "Even if it was barbed wire."

He walked back to the bed and sat down. After they had finished examining him, the French doctors had brought him fresh clothes. Military clothes, he noticed. Combat jacket and trousers.

He hoped they weren't trying to tell him something.

"I've got three questions," he said. "But let's start with the big one. I called for help two days ago. Where were you?"

"I'm very sorry, Alex," Mrs Jones said. "There were ... logistical problems."

"Yes? Well, while you were having your logistical problems, Dr Grief was getting ready to cut me up!"

"We couldn't just storm the academy. That could have got you killed. It could have got you all killed. We had to move in slowly. Try and work out what was going on. How do you think we found you so quickly?"

"That was my second question."

Mrs Jones shrugged. "We've had people in the mountains ever since we got your signal. They've been closing in on the academy. They heard the machine-gun fire when the snowmobiles were chasing you and followed you down on skis. They saw what happened with the train and radioed for help."

"All right. So why all the business with the funeral? Why do you want Dr Grief to think I'm dead?"

"That's simple, Alex. From what you've told

us, he's keeping fifteen boys prisoner in the academy. These are the boys that he plans to replace." She shook her head. "I have to say, it's the most incredible thing I've ever heard. And I wouldn't have believed it if I'd heard it from anyone else except you."

"You're too kind," Alex muttered.

"If Dr Grief thought you'd survived last night, the first thing he would do is kill every one of those boys. Or perhaps he'd use them as hostages. We only had one hope if we were going to take him by surprise. He had to believe you were dead."

"You're going to take him by surprise?"

"We're going in tonight. I told you, we've assembled an attack squad here in Grenoble. They were up in the mountains last night. They plan to set off as soon as it's dark. They're armed and they're experienced." Mrs Jones hesitated. "There's just one thing they don't have."

"And what's that?" Alex asked, feeling a sudden sense of unease.

"They need someone who knows the building," Mrs Jones said. "The library, the secret lift, the placement of the guards, the passage with the cells—"

"No way!" Alex exclaimed. Now he understood

the military clothes. "Forget it! I'm not going back up there! I almost got killed trying to get away! Do you think I'm mad?"

"Alex, you'll be looked after. You'll be completely safe—"

"No!"

Mrs Jones nodded. "All right. I can understand your feelings. But there's someone I want you to meet."

As if on cue, there was a knock on the door and it opened to reveal a young man, also in combat dress. The man was well-built with black hair, square shoulders and a dark, watchful face. He was in his late twenties. He saw Alex and shook his head. "Well, well, well. There's a turn up for the books," he said. "How's it going, Cub?"

Alex recognized him at once. It was the soldier he had known as Wolf. When MI6 had sent him for eleven days' SAS training in Wales, Wolf had been in charge of his unit. If training had been hell, Wolf had only made it worse, picking on Alex from the start and almost getting him thrown out. In the end though, it had been Wolf who had nearly lost his place with the SAS and Alex who had saved him. But Alex still wasn't sure where that left him, and the other man was giving nothing away.

"Wolf!" Alex said.

"I heard you got busted up." Wolf shrugged. "I'm sorry. I forgot the flowers and the bunch of grapes."

"What are you doing here?" Alex asked.

"They called me in to clear up the mess you left behind you."

"So where were you when I was being chased down the mountain?"

"It seems you were doing fine on your own."

Mrs Jones took over. "Alex has done a very good job up to now," she said. "But the fact is that there are fifteen young prisoners up at Point Blanc and our first priority must be to save them. From what Alex has told us, we know there are about thirty guards in and around the school. The only chance those boys have is for an SAS unit to break in. It's happening tonight." She turned to Alex. "The unit will be commanded by Wolf."

The SAS never use rank when they are on active service. Mrs Jones was careful only to use Wolf's code-name.

"Where does the boy come into this?" Wolf demanded.

"He knows the school. He knows the position of the guards and the location of the prison cells.

He can lead you to the lift—"

"He can tell us everything we need to know here and now," Wolf interrupted. He turned to Mrs Jones. "We don't need a kid," he said. "He's just going to be baggage. We're going in on skis. Maybe there'll be blood. I can't waste one of my men holding his hand—"

"I don't need to have my hand held," Alex retorted angrily. "She's right. I know more about Point Blanc than any of you. I've been there – and got out of there, no thanks to you. Also, I've met some of those boys. One of them is a friend of mine. I promised I'd help him and I will."

"Not if you get killed."

"I can look after myself."

"Then it's agreed," Mrs Jones said. "Alex will lead you in there but then will take no further part in the operation. And as for his safety, Wolf, I hold you personally responsible."

"Personally responsible. Right," Wolf growled.

Alex couldn't resist a smile. He'd held his ground and he'd be going back in with the SAS. Then he realized. A few moments ago, he'd been arguing violently against doing just that. He glanced at Mrs Jones. She'd manipulated him, of course, bringing Wolf into the room. And she knew it.

Wolf nodded. "All right, Cub," he said. "Looks like you're in. Let's go play."

"Sure, Wolf," Alex sighed. "Let's go play."

NIGHT RAID

They came skiing down from the mountain.
There were seven of them. Wolf was the leader.
Alex was at his side. The other five men followed.
They had changed into white trousers, jackets
and hoods – camouflage that would help them
blend into the snow. A helicopter had dropped
them two kilometres north of and two hundred
metres above Point Blanc and, equipped with
night vision goggles, they had quickly made their
way down. The weather had settled again. The
moon was out. Despite himself, Alex enjoyed the
journey, the whisper of the skis cutting through
the ice, the empty mountainside bathed in white
light. And he was part of a crack SAS unit. He
felt safe.

But then the academy loomed up below him,

and once again he shivered. Before they had left, he had asked for a gun – but Wolf had shaken his head.

"I'm sorry, Cub. It's orders. You get us in, then you get out of sight."

There were no lights showing in the building. The helicopter crouched on the helipad like a glittering insect. The ski-jump stood to one side, dark and forgotten. There was nobody in sight. Wolf held up a hand and they slid to a halt.

"Guards?" he whispered.

"Two patrolling. One on the roof."

"Let's take him out first."

Mrs Jones had made her instructions clear. There was to be no bloodshed unless absolutely necessary. The mission was to get the boys out. The SAS could take care of Dr Grief, Mrs Stellenbosch and the guards at a later date.

Now Wolf held out a hand and one of the other men passed him something. It was a crossbow – not the medieval sort but a sophisticated, high-tech weapon with a microflite aluminium barrel and laser scope. He loaded it with an anaesthetic dart, lifted it up and took aim. Alex saw him smile to himself. Then his finger curled and the dart flashed across the night, travelling at one hundred metres a second. There was a faint sound from the roof of the academy. It was as if someone had coughed. Wolf lowered the crossbow.

"One down," he said.

"Sure," Alex muttered. "And about twenty-nine to go."

Wolf signalled and they continued down, more slowly now. They were about twenty metres from the school when they saw the main door open. Two men walked out, machine-guns hanging from their shoulders. As one, the SAS men veered to the right, disappearing round the side of the school. They stopped within reach of the wall, dropping down to lie flat on their stomachs. Two of the men had moved slightly ahead. Alex noticed that they had kicked off their skis at the very same moment they had come to a halt.

The two guards approached. One of them was talking quietly in German. Alex's face was half buried in the snow. He knew that the combat clothes would make them invisible. He half-lifted his head just in time to see two figures rise out of the ground like ghosts from the grave. Two coshes swung in the moonlight. The guards crumpled. In seconds they were tied up and gagged. They wouldn't be going anywhere that night.

Wolf signalled again. The men got up and ran

forward, making for the main door. Alex hastily pulled his own skis off and followed. They reached the door in a line, their backs against the wall. Wolf looked inside to check that it was safe. He nodded. They went in.

They were in the hall with the stone dragons and the animal heads. Alex found himself next to Wolf and quickly gave him his bearings, pointing out the different rooms.

"The library?" Wolf whispered. He was totally serious now. Alex could see the tension in his eyes.

"Through here."

Wolf took a step forward, then crouched down, his hand whipping into one of the pouches of his jacket. Another guard had appeared, patrolling the lower corridor. Dr Grief was taking no more chances. Wolf waited until the man had gone past, then nodded. One of the other SAS men went after him. Alex heard a thud and the clatter of a gun dropping.

"So far, so good," Wolf whispered.

They went into the library. Alex showed Wolf how to summon the lift and Wolf whistled softly as the suit of armour smoothly divided into two parts. "This is quite a place," he muttered.

"Are you going up or down?"

"Down. Let's make sure the kids are all right."

There was just room for all seven of them in the lift. Alex had warned Wolf about the guard at the table, within sight of the lift, and Wolf took no chances – he came out firing. In fact, there were two guards there. One of them was holding a mug of coffee, the other lighting a cigarette. Wolf fired twice. Two more anaesthetic darts travelled the short distance along the corridor and found their targets. Again, it had all happened in almost total silence. The two guards collapsed and lay still. The SAS men stepped out into the corridor.

Suddenly Alex remembered. He was angry with himself for not mentioning it before. "You can't go into the cells," he whispered. "They're wired up for sound."

Wolf nodded. "Show me!"

Alex showed Wolf the passage with the steel doors. Wolf pointed to one of the men. "I want you to stay here. If we're found, this is the first place Grief will come."

The man nodded. He understood. The rest of them went back to the lift, up to the library and out into the hall.

Wolf turned to Alex. "We're going to have to deactivate the alarm," he explained. "Do you have any idea—?"

"This way. Grief's private rooms are on the other side..."

But before he could finish, three more guards appeared, walking down the passageway. Wolf shot one of them – another anaesthetic dart – and one of his men took out the other two. But this time they were a fraction of a second too slow. Alex saw one of the guards bring his gun round. He was probably unconscious before he managed to fire. But at the last moment, his finger tightened on the trigger. Bullets sprayed upwards, smashing into the ceiling, bringing plaster and wood splinters showering down. Nobody had been hit, but the damage had been done. The lights flashed on. An alarm began to ring.

Twenty metres away, a door opened and more guards poured through.

"Down!" Wolf shouted.

He had produced a grenade. He tugged the pin out and threw it. Alex hit the ground and a second later there was a soft explosion as a great cloud of tear gas filled the far end of the passage. The guards staggered, blind and helpless. The SAS men quickly took them out.

Wolf grabbed hold of Alex and dragged him close. "Find somewhere to hide!" he shouted. "You've got us in. We'll do the rest now."

"Give me a gun!" Alex shouted back. Some of the gas had reached him and he could feel his eyes burning.

"No. I've got orders. At the first sign of trouble, you're to get out of the way. Find somewhere safe. We'll come for you later."

"Wolf...!"

But Wolf was already up and running. Alex heard machine-gun fire coming from somewhere below. So Wolf had been right. One of the guards had been sent to take care of the prisoners – but there had been an SAS man waiting for him. And now the rules had changed. The SAS couldn't afford to risk the lives of the prisoners. There was going to be bloodshed. Alex could only imagine the battle that must be taking place. But he was to be no part of it. His job was to hide.

More explosions. More gunfire. There was a bitter taste in Alex's mouth as he made his way back to the stairs. It was typical of MI6. Half the time they would happily get him killed. The other half they treated him like a child.

Suddenly a guard appeared, running towards the sound of the fighting. Alex's eyes were still smarting from the gas and now he made use of it. He brought his hand up to his face, pretending to cry. The guard saw a fourteen-year-old boy in tears. He stopped. At that moment Alex twisted round on his left foot, driving the upper part of his right foot sideways into the man's stomach – the roundhouse kick or *mawashi geri* he had learned in karate. The guard didn't even have time to cry out. His eyes rolled and he went limp. Alex felt a little better after that.

But there was still nothing more for him to do. There was another round of gunfire, then the quiet blast of a second gas grenade. Alex went into the dining-room. From here he could look out through the windows at the side of the building and the helipad above. He noticed that the blades of the helicopter were turning. Somebody was inside it. He moved closer to the window. It was Dr Grief! He had to let Wolf know.

He turned round.

Mrs Stellenbosch was standing in front of him.

He had never seen her look less human. Her entire face was contorted with anger, her lips rolled outwards, her eyes ablaze.

"You didn't die!" she exclaimed. "You're still alive!" Her voice was almost a whine, as if somehow none of it had been fair. "You brought them here. You ruined everything!"

"That's my job," Alex said.

"What was it that made me look in here?" Mrs

Stellenbosch giggled to herself. Alex could see what little sanity she had left was slipping away. "Well, at least this is one bit of business I'm finally going to be able to finish."

Alex tensed himself, feet apart, centre of gravity low. Just like he had been taught. But it was useless. Mrs Stellenbosch lurched into him, moving with frightening speed. It was like being run over by a bus. Alex felt the full impact of her body weight, then cried out as two massive hands seized hold of him and threw him head first across the room. He crashed into a table, knocking it over, then rolled out of the way as Mrs Stellenbosch followed up her first attack, lashing out with a kick that would have taken his head off his shoulders if it hadn't missed by less than a centimetre.

He scrambled to his feet and stood there, panting for breath. For a moment his vision was blurred. Blood trickled out of the corner of his mouth. Mrs Stellenbosch charged again. Alex threw himself forward, using another of the tables for leverage. His feet swung round, scything through the air, both his heels catching her on the back of the head. Anyone else would have been knocked out by the blow. But although Alex felt the jolt of it running all the way up his body, Mrs Stellenbosch hardly faltered. As Alex left the table, her hands swung down, smashing through the thick wood. The table fell apart and she walked through it, grabbing him again, this time by the neck. Alex felt his feet leave the floor. With a grunt she hurled him against the wall. Alex yelled, wondering if his back had been broken. He slid to the floor. He couldn't move.

Mrs Stellenbosch stopped, breathing heavily. She glanced out of the window. The helicopter's blades were at full speed now. The helicopter rocked forward then rose into the air. It was time to go.

She reached down and picked up her handbag. She took out a gun and aimed at Alex. Alex stared at her. There was nothing he could do.

Mrs Stellenbosch smiled. "And this is *my* job," she said.

The dining-room door swung open.

"Alex!" It was Wolf. He was holding a machine-gun.

Mrs Stellenbosch lifted the gun up and fired three shots. Each one of them found its target. Wolf was hit in the shoulder, the arm and the chest. But even as he fell back, he opened fire himself. The heavy bullets slammed into Mrs Stellenbosch. She was hurled backwards into the window, which smashed behind her. With a scream she disappeared out into the night and the snow, head first, her heavy stockinged legs trailing behind her.

The shock of what had happened gave Alex new strength. He got to his feet and ran over to Wolf. The SAS man wasn't dead but he was badly hurt, his breath rattling.

"I'm OK," he managed to say. "Came looking for you. Glad I found you."

"Wolf..."

"OK." He tapped at his chest and Alex saw that he was wearing body armour under his jacket. There was blood coming from his arm but the other two bullets hadn't reached him. "Grief..." he said.

Wolf gestured and Alex looked round. The helicopter had left its launch pad. It was flying low outside the academy. Alex saw Dr Grief in the pilot's seat. He had a gun. He fired. There was a yell and a body fell from somewhere above. One of the SAS men.

Suddenly Alex was angry. Grief was a freak, a monster. He was responsible for all this – and he was going to get away. Not knowing what he was doing, he snatched up Wolf's gun and ran through the broken window, past the dead body of Mrs

Stellenbosch and into the night. He tried to aim. The blades of the helicopter were whipping up the surface snow, blinding him, but he pointed the gun up and fired. Nothing happened. He pulled the trigger again. Still nothing. Either Wolf had used all his ammunition or the gun had jammed.

Dr Grief pulled at the controls and the helicopter banked away, following the slope of the mountain. It was too late. Nothing could stop him.

Unless...

Alex threw down the gun and ran forward. There was a snowmobile lying idle a few metres away, its engine still running. The man who had been riding it was lying face down in the snow. Alex leapt onto the seat and turned the throttle full on. The snowmobile roared away, skimming over the ice, following the path of the helicopter.

Dr Grief saw him. The helicopter slowed and turned. Grief raised a hand – waving goodbye.

Alex caught sight of the red spectacles, the slender fingers raised in one last gesture of defiance. With his hands gripping the handlebars Alex stood up on the foot-grips, tensing himself for what he knew he had to do. The helicopter moved away again, gaining altitude. In front of

Alex, the ski-jump loomed up. He was travelling at seventy, eighty kilometres an hour, snow and wind rushing past him. Ahead of him there was a wooden barrier shaped like a cross.

Alex smashed through it, then threw himself off.

The snowmobile plunged down, its engine screaming.

Alex rolled over and over in the snow, ice and wood splinters in his eyes and mouth. He managed to get to his knees.

The snowmobile reached the end of the ski-jump.

Alex watched it rocket into the air, propelled by the huge metal slide.

In the helicopter Dr Grief just had time to see 225 kilograms of solid steel come hurtling towards him out of the night, its headlights blazing, its engine still screaming. His eyes, bright red, opened wide in shock.

The explosion lit up the entire mountain. The snowmobile had become a torpedo and it hit its target with perfect accuracy. The helicopter disappeared in a huge fireball, then plunged down. It was still burning when it hit the ground.

Behind him, Alex became aware that the shooting had stopped. The battle was over. He walked slowly back to the academy, shivering suddenly in the cold night air. As he approached, a man appeared at the broken window and waved. It was Wolf, propping himself against the wall but still very much alive. Alex went over to him.

"What happened to Grief?" he asked.

"It looks like I sleighed him," Alex replied.

On the slopes, the wreckage of the helicopter flickered and burned as the morning sun began to rise.

DEAD RINGER

A few days later, Alex found himself sitting opposite Alan Blunt in the faceless office in Liverpool Street, with Mrs Jones twisting another sweet between her fingers. It was 1 May, a bank holiday in England – but somehow he knew that holidays never came to the building that called itself the Royal & General bank. Even the spring seemed to have stopped at the window. Outside, the sun was shining. Inside, there were only shadows.

"It seems that once again we owe you a debt of thanks," Blunt was saying.

"You don't owe me anything," Alex said.

Blunt looked genuinely puzzled. "You have quite possibly changed the future of this planet," he said. "Of course, Grief's plan was monstrous, crazy. But the fact remains that his..." He searched for a word to describe the test-tube creations that had been sent out of Point Blanc. "...his *offspring* could have caused a great many problems. At the very least they would have had money. God knows what they would have got up to had they remained undiscovered."

"What's happened to them?" Alex asked.

"We've traced all fifteen of them and we have them under lock and key," Mrs Jones answered. "They were quietly arrested by the intelligence services of each country where they lived. We'll take care of them."

Alex shivered. He had a feeling he knew what Mrs Jones meant by those last words. And he was certain that nobody would ever see the fifteen Grief replicas again.

"Once again, we've had to hush this up," Blunt continued. "This whole business of ... cloning. It causes a great deal of public disquiet. Sheep are one thing – but human beings!" He coughed. "The families involved in this business have no desire for publicity, so they won't be talking. They're just glad to have their real sons returned to them. The same, of course, goes for you, Alex. You've already signed the Official Secrets Act. I'm sure we can trust you to be discreet."

270

There was a moment's pause. Mrs Jones looked carefully at Alex. She had to admit that she was worried about him. She knew everything that had happened at Point Blanc – how close he had come to a horrible death, only to be sent back into the academy for a second time. The boy who had come back from the French Alps was different to the boy who had left. There was a coldness about him, as tangible as the mountain snow.

"You did very well, Alex," she said.

"How is Wolf?" Alex asked.

"He's fine. He's still in hospital but the doctors say he'll make a complete recovery. We hope to have him back on operations in a few weeks."

"That's good."

"We only had one fatality in the raid on Point Blanc. That was the man you saw falling from the roof. Wolf and another man were injured. Otherwise, it was a complete success." She paused. "Is there anything else you want to know?"

"No." Alex shook his head. He stood up. "You left me in there," he said. "I called for help and you didn't come. Grief was going to kill me, but you didn't care."

"That's not true, Alex!" Mrs Jones looked at Blunt for support but he didn't meet her eyes. "There were difficulties..."

"It doesn't matter. I just want you to know that I've had enough. I don't want to be a spy any more and if you ask me again, I'll refuse. I know you think you can blackmail me. But I know too much about you now, so that won't work any more." He walked over to the door. "I used to think that being a spy would be exciting and special ... like in the films. But you just used me. In a way, the two of you are as bad as Grief. You'll do anything to get what you want. Well, I want to go back to school. Next time, you can do it without me."

There was a long silence after Alex had left. At last, Blunt spoke. "He'll be back," he said.

Mrs Jones raised an eyebrow. "You really think so?"

"He's too good at what he does ... too good at the job. And it's in his blood." He stood up. "It's rather odd," he said. "Most schoolboys dream of being spies. With Alex, we have a spy who dreams of being a schoolboy."

"Will you really use him again?" Mrs Jones asked.

"Of course. There was a file that came in only this morning. An interesting situation in the Zagros Mountains of Iraq. Alex may be the only answer." He smiled at his number two. "We'll give him a while to settle down and then we'll call him."

"He won't answer."

"We'll see," Blunt said.

Alex walked home from the bus-stop and let himself into the elegant Chelsea house that he shared with his housekeeper and closest friend, Jack Starbright. Alex had already told Jack where he had been and what he had been doing, but the two of them had made an agreement never to discuss his involvement with MI6. She didn't like it and she worried about him. But at the end of the day they both knew there was nothing more to be said.

She seemed surprised to see him. "I thought you'd just gone out," she said.

"No."

"Did you get the message by the phone?"

"What message?"

"Mr Bray wants to see you this afternoon. Three o'clock at the school."

Henry Bray was the head-teacher at Brookland. Alex wasn't surprised by the summons. Bray was the sort of head who managed to run a busy comprehensive and still find time to take a personal interest in every pupil who went there. He had been worried by Alex's long absences. So he had called a meeting.

"Do you want lunch?" Jack asked.

"No thanks." Alex knew that he would have to pretend he had been ill again. Doubtless MI6 would produce another doctor's note in due course. But the thought of lying to his headteacher spoiled his appetite.

He set off an hour later, taking his bicycle, which had been returned to the house by the Putney police. He cycled slowly. It was good to be back in London, to be surrounded by normal life. He turned off the King's Road and pedalled down the side road where – it felt like a month ago – he had followed the man in the white Skoda. The school loomed up ahead of him. It was empty now and would remain so until the summer term.

But as Alex arrived, he saw a figure walking across the yard to the school gates and recognized Mr Lee, the elderly school caretaker.

"You again!"

"Hello, Bernie," Alex said. That was what everyone called him.

"On your way to see Mr Bray?"

"Yeah."

The caretaker shook his head. "He never told me he was going to be here today. But he never tells me anything! I'm just going down to the shops. I'll be back at five to lock up – so make sure you're out by then."

"Right, Bernie."

There was nobody in the playground. It felt strange, walking across the tarmac on his own. The school seemed bigger with nobody there, the yard stretching out too far between the red-brick buildings, with the sun beating down, reflecting off the windows. Alex was dazzled. He had never seen the place so empty and so quiet. The grass on the playing-fields looked almost too green. Any school without schoolchildren has its own peculiar atmosphere and Brookland was no exception.

Mr Bray had an office in D block, which was next to the science building. Alex reached the swing-doors and opened them. The walls here would normally be covered in posters but they had all been taken down at the end of term. Everything was blank, off-white. There was another door open to one side. Bernie had been cleaning the main laboratory. He had rested his mop and bucket to one side when he'd gone to the shops – to pick up twenty cigarettes, Alex presumed. The man had been a chain smoker all his life and Alex knew he'd die with a cigarette between his lips.

Alex climbed up the stairs, his heels rapping against the stone surface. He reached a corridor – left for biology, right for physics – and continued straight ahead. A second corridor, with full-length windows on both sides, led into D block. Bray's study was directly ahead of him. He stopped at the door, vaguely wondering if he should have smartened up for the meeting. Bray was always snapping at boys with their shirts hanging out or ties crooked. Alex was wearing a denim jacket, T-shirt, jeans and Nike trainers – the same clothes he had worn that morning at MI6. His hair was still too short for his liking, although it had begun to grow back. All in all, he still looked like a juvenile delinquent – but it was too late now. And anyway, Bray didn't want to see him to discuss his appearance. His non-appearance at school was more to the point.

He knocked on the door.

"Come in!" a voice called.

Alex opened the door and walked into the head-teacher's study, a cluttered room with views over the playground. There was a desk, piled high with papers, and a black leather chair with its back towards the door. A cabinet full of trophies stood against one wall. The others were mainly lined with books.

"You wanted to see me," Alex said.

The chair turned slowly round.

Alex froze.

It wasn't Henry Bray sitting behind the desk.

It was himself.

He was looking at a fourteen-year-old boy with fair hair cut very short, brown eyes and a slim, pale face. The boy was even dressed identically to him. It took Alex what felt like an eternity to accept what he was seeing. He was standing in a room looking at himself sitting in a chair. The boy *was* him.

With just one difference. The boy was holding a gun.

"Sit down," he said.

Alex didn't move. He knew what he was facing and he was angry with himself for not having expected it. When he had been handcuffed at the academy, Dr Grief had boasted to him that he had cloned himself sixteen times. But that morning Mrs Jones had traced "all fifteen of them". That left one spare – one boy waiting to take his place in the family of Sir David Friend. Alex had glimpsed him while he was at the academy. Now he remembered the figure with the white mask, watching him from a window as he walked over to the ski-jump. The white mask had been bandages. The new Alex had been spying on him as he recovered from the plastic surgery that had made the two of them identical.

And even today there had been clues. Perhaps it had been the heat of the sun – or the fall-out from his visit to MI6. But he had been too wrapped up in his own thoughts to see them: Jack, when he got home – "I thought you'd just gone out"; Bernie, at the gate – "You again!"

They had both thought they'd just seen him. And in a sense, they had. They had seen the boy sitting opposite him now. The boy who was aiming a gun at his heart.

"I've been looking forward to this," the other boy said. Despite the hatred in his voice, Alex couldn't help marvelling. The voice wasn't the same as his. The boy hadn't had enough time to get it right. But otherwise he was a dead ringer.

"What are you doing here?" Alex said. "It's all over. The Gemini Project is finished. You might as well turn yourself in. You need help."

"I need just one thing," the second Alex sneered. "I need to see you dead. I'm going to shoot you. I'm going to do it now. You killed my father!"

"Your father was a test-tube," Alex said. "You never had a mother or a father. You're a freak.

Hand-made in the Alps ... like a cuckoo clock. What are you going to do when you've killed me? Take my place? You wouldn't last a week. You may look like me, but too many people know what Grief was trying to do. And I'm sorry, but you've got *fake* written all over you."

"We would have had everything! We would have had the whole world!" The replica Alex almost screamed the words and for a moment Alex thought he heard Dr Grief somewhere in there, blaming him from beyond the grave. But then the creature in front of him *was* Dr Grief ... or part of him. "I don't care what happens to me," he went on, "just so long as you're dead."

The hand with the gun stretched out. The barrel was pointing at him. Alex looked the boy straight in the eye.

And he saw the hesitation.

The fake Alex couldn't quite bring himself to do it. They were too similar. The same height, the same build – the same *face*. For the other boy, it would be like shooting himself. Alex still hadn't closed the door. He threw himself backwards, out into the corridor. At the same time, the gun went off, the bullet exploding millimetres above his head and crashing into the far wall. Alex hit the ground on his back and rolled out of the doorway as a second bullet slammed into the floor. And then he was running, putting as much space between himself and his double as he could.

There was a third shot as he sprinted down the corridor and the window next to him shattered, glass showering down. Alex reached the stairs and took them three at a time, afraid that he would trip and break an ankle. But then he was at the bottom, heading for the main door, swerving only when he realized that he would make too easy a target as he crossed the playground. Instead he dived into the laboratory, almost falling head first over Bernie's bucket and mop.

The laboratory was long and rectangular, divided into work stations with Bunsen burners, flasks and dozens of bottles of chemicals spread out on shelves that stretched the full length of the room. There was another door at the far end. Alex dived behind the furthest desk. Would his double have seen him come in? Might he be looking for him, even now, out in the yard?

Cautiously Alex poked his head over the surface, then ducked down as four bullets ricocheted around him, splintering the wood and smashing one of the gas pipes. Alex heard the hiss of escaping gas, then there was another gunshot and an explosion that hurled him backwards, sprawling onto the floor. The last bullet had ignited the gas. Flames leapt up, licking at the ceiling. Then the sprinkler system went off, spraying the entire room. Alex tracked back on his hands and feet, searching for shelter behind fire and water, hoping that the other Alex would be blinded. His shoulders hit the far door. He scrambled to his feet. There was another shot. But then he was through – with another corridor and a second flight of stairs straight ahead.

The stairs led nowhere. He was halfway up before he remembered. There was a single classroom at the top, used for biology. It had a spiral staircase leading to the roof. The school had so little land that they'd planned to build a roof garden. Then they'd run out of money. There were a couple of greenhouses. Nothing more.

There was no way down! Alex looked over his shoulder and saw the other Alex reloading his gun, already on his way up. He had no choice. He had to continue even though he knew that he was soon going to be trapped.

He reached the biology classroom and slammed the door shut behind him. There was no lock and the tables were all bolted into the floor, otherwise he might have been able to make a barricade. The spiral staircase was ahead of him. He ran up it without stopping, through another door and out onto the roof. Alex stopped to catch his breath and see what he could do next.

He was standing on a wide, flat area with a fence running all the way round. There were half a dozen terracotta pots filled with earth. A few plants sprouted out, looking more dead than alive. Alex sniffed the air. Smoke was curling up from the windows two floors below and he realized that the sprinkler system had failed to put out the fire. He thought of the gas pouring into the room and the chemicals stacked up on the shelves. He could be standing on a time-bomb! He had to find a way down.

But then he heard feet on metal and realized that his double had reached the top of the spiral staircase. Alex ducked behind one of the greenhouses. The door crashed open.

Smoke followed the fake Alex out onto the roof. He took a step forward. Now Alex was behind him.

"Where are you?" shouted the double. His hair was soaked and his face contorted with anger.

Alex knew his moment had come. He would never have a better chance. He ran forward. The other Alex twisted round and fired. The bullet creased his shoulder, a molten sword drawn across his flesh. But then he had reached his replica, grabbing him around the neck with one hand and seizing hold of his wrist with the other, forcing the gun away. There was a huge explosion in the laboratory below and the entire building shook, but neither of the boys seemed to notice it. They were locked in an embrace, two reflections that had become tangled up in the mirror, the gun over their heads, fighting for control.

The flames were tearing through the building. Fed by a variety of chemicals, they burst through the roof, melting the asphalt. In the far distance the scream of fire engines penetrated the sun-filled air. Alex pulled with all his strength, trying to bring the gun down. The other Alex clawed at him, swearing – not in English but in Afrikaans.

The end came very suddenly.

The gun twisted and fell to the ground.

One Alex lashed out, knocking the other down, then dived for the gun.

There was another explosion and a sheet of chemical flame leapt up. A crater had suddenly appeared in the roof, swallowing up the gun. The boy saw it too late and fell through. With a yell, he disappeared into the smoke and fire.

One Alex Rider walked over to the hole and looked down.

The other Alex Rider lay on his back, two floors below. He wasn't moving. The flames were closing in.

The first fire engines had arrived at the school. A ladder slanted up towards the roof.

A boy with short fair hair and brown eyes, wearing a denim jacket, T-shirt and jeans, walked to the edge of the roof and began to climb down.

Read the next mission in the Alex Rider series: Skeleton Key

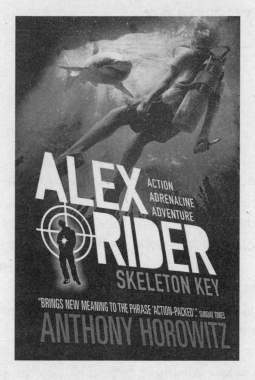

Sharks. Nuclear Bombs. Alex is in deep water.

Turn over for a short taster...

IN THE DARK

Night came quickly to Skeleton Key.

The sun hovered briefly on the horizon, then dipped below. At once, the clouds rolled in – first red, then mauve, silver, green and black as if all the colours in the world were being sucked into a vast melting pot. A single frigate bird soared over the mangroves, its own colours lost in the chaos behind it. The air was close. Rain hung waiting. There was going to be a storm.

The single engine Cessna Skyhawk SP circled twice before coming in to land. It was the sort of plane that would barely have been noticed, flying in this part of the world. That was why it had been chosen. If anyone had been curious enough to check the registration number printed under the wing, they would have learned that this plane belonged to a photographic company based in Jamaica. This was not true. There was no company and it was already too dark to take photographs.

There were three men in the aircraft. They were all dark skinned, wearing faded jeans and loose, open-neck shirts. The pilot had long black hair, deep brown eyes and a thin scar running down the side of his face. He had met his two passengers only that afternoon. They had introduced themselves as Carlo and Marc but he doubted these were their real names. He knew that their journey had begun a long time ago, somewhere in Eastern Europe. He knew that this short flight was the last leg. He knew what they were carrying. Already, he knew too much.

The pilot glanced down at the multifunction display in the control panel. The illuminated computer screen was warning him of the storm that was closing in. That didn't worry him. Low clouds and rain gave him cover. The authorities were less vigilant during a storm. Even so, he was nervous. He had flown into Cuba many times, but never here. And tonight he would have preferred to have been going almost anywhere else.

Cayo Esqueleto. Skeleton Key.

There it was, stretching out before him, thirty-eight kilometres long and nine kilometres across at its widest point. The sea around it, which had been an extraordinary, brilliant blue until a few minutes ago, had suddenly darkened, as if someone had thrown a switch. Over to the west, he could make out the twinkling lights of Puerto Madre, the island's second biggest town. The main airport was further north, outside the capital of Santiago. But that wasn't where he was heading. He pressed on the joystick and the plane veered to the right, circling over the forests and mangrove swamps that surrounded the old, abandoned airport at the bottom end of the island.

The Cessna had been equipped with a thermal intensifier, similar to the sort used in American spy satellites. He flicked a switch and glanced at the display. A few birds appeared as tiny pinpricks of red. There were more dots pulsating in the swamp. Crocodiles or perhaps manatees. And a single dot about twenty metres from the runway. He turned to speak to the man called Carlo but there was no need. Carlo was already leaning over his shoulder, staring at the screen.

Carlo nodded. There was only one man waiting for them, as agreed. Anyone hiding within a few hundred metres of the airstrip would have shown up. It was safe to land.

The pilot looked out of the window and there was the runway. It was a rough strip of land on the edge of the coast, hacked out of the jungle and running parallel with the sea. The pilot would have missed it altogether in the dying light but for the two lines of electric bulbs burning at ground level, outlining the path for the plane.

The Cessna swooped out of the sky. At the last minute it was buffeted about by a sudden, damp squall that had been sent to try the pilot's nerve. The pilot didn't blink and a moment later the wheels hit the ground and the plane was bouncing and shuddering along, dead centre between the two rows of lights. He was grateful they were there. The mangroves – thick bushes, half-floating on pools of stagnant water – came almost to the edge of the runway. Go even a couple of metres in the wrong direction and a wheel might snag. It would be enough to destroy the plane.

The pilot flicked switches. The engine died and the twin-bladed propellers slowed down and came to a halt. He looked out of the window. There was a jeep parked next to one of the buildings and it was here that the single man – the red dot on his screen – was waiting. He turned to his passengers.

"He's there."

The older of the two men nodded. Carlo was about thirty years old with black, curly hair. He hadn't shaved. Stubble the colour of cigarette ash clung to his jaw. He turned to the other passenger. "Marc? Are you ready?"

The man who called himself Marc could have been Carlo's younger brother. He was barely twenty-five and although he was trying not to show it, he was scared. There was sweat on the side of his face, glowing green as it caught the light from the control panel. He reached behind him and took out a gun, a German-built 10mm Glock automatic. He checked it was loaded, then slipped it into the waistband at the back of his trousers, under his shirt.

"I'm ready," he said.

"There is only him. There are two of us." Carlo tried to reassure Marc. Or perhaps he was trying to reassure himself. "We're both armed. There is nothing he can do."

"Then let's go."

Carlo turned to the pilot. "Have the plane ready," he commanded. "When we walk back, I will give you a sign." He raised a hand, one finger and thumb forming an O. "That is the signal that our business has been successfully concluded.

Start the engine at that time. We don't want to stay here one second longer than we have to."

They got out of the plane. There was a thin layer of gravel on the runway which crunched beneath their combat boots as they walked round the side to the cargo door. They could feel the sullen heat in the air, the heaviness of the night sky. The island seemed to be holding its breath. Carlo reached up and opened a door. In the back of the plane was a black container, about one metre by two. With difficulty, he and Marc lowered it to the ground.

The younger man looked up. The lights on the landing strip dazzled him but he could just make out a figure standing still as a statue beside the jeep, waiting for them to approach. He hadn't moved since the plane had landed. "Why doesn't he come to us?" he asked.

Carlo spat and said nothing.

There were two handles, one on either side of the container. The two men carried it between them, walking awkwardly, bending over their load. It took them a long time to reach the jeep. But at last they were there. For a second time, they set the box down.

Carlo straightened up, rubbing his palms on the side of his jeans. "Good evening, General," he said. He was speaking in English. This was not his native language. Nor was it the general's. But it was the only language they had in common.

"Good evening." The general did not bother with names that he knew would be false anyway. "You had no trouble getting here?"

"No trouble at all, General."

"You have it?"

"One kilogram of weapons grade uranium. Sufficient to build a bomb powerful enough to destroy a city. I would be interested to know which city you have in mind."

General Alexei Sarov took a step forward and the lights from the runway illuminated him. He was not a big man, yet there was something about him that radiated power and control. He still carried with him his years in the army. They could be seen in his close-cut, iron grey hair, his watchful pale blue eyes, his almost emotionless face. They were there in the very way he carried himself. He was perfectly poised; relaxed and wary at the same time. General Sarov was sixty-two years old but looked twenty years younger. He was dressed in a dark suit, a white shirt and a narrow dark blue tie. In the damp heat of the evening, his clothes should have been creased. He should have been sweating. But to look at him, he could have just stepped out of an air-conditioned room.

He crouched down beside the container, at the same time producing a small device from his pocket. It looked like a car cigarette lighter with a dial attached. He found a socket in the side of the box and plugged the device in. Briefly, he examined the dial. He nodded. It was satisfactory.

"You have the rest of the money?" Carlo asked.

"Of course." The general straightened up and walked over to the jeep. Carlo and Marc tensed themselves – this was the moment when he might produce a gun. But when he turned round he was holding a black leather attaché-case. He flicked the locks and opened it. The case was filled with banknotes: one hundred dollar bills neatly banded together in packets of fifty. One hundred packets in all. A total of half a million dollars. More money than Carlo had ever seen in his life.

But still not enough.

"We've had a problem," Carlo said.

"Yes?" Sarov did not sound surprised.

Marc could feel the sweat as it drew a comma down the side of his neck. A mosquito was whining in his ear but he resisted the urge to slap it. This was what he had been waiting for. He was standing a few steps away, his hands hanging limply by his side. Slowly, he allowed them to creep behind him, closer to the concealed gun. He glanced at the ruined buildings. One might once have been a control tower. The other looked like a customs shed. Both of them were broken and empty, the brickwork crumbling, the windows smashed. Could there be someone hiding there? No. The thermal intensifier would have shown them. They were alone.

"The cost of the uranium." Carlo shrugged. "Our friend in Miami sends his apologies. But there are new security systems all over the world. Smuggling – particularly this sort of thing – has become much more difficult. And that's meant extra expense."

"How much extra expense?"

"A quarter of a million dollars."

"That's unfortunate."

"Unfortunate for you, General. You're the one who has to pay."

Sarov considered. "We had an agreement," he said.

"Our friend in Miami hoped you'd understand."

There was a long silence. Marc's fingers reached out behind his back, closing around the Glock automatic. But then Sarov nodded. "I will have to raise the money," he said.

"You can have it transferred to the same account that we used before," Carlo said. "But I have to warn you, General. If the money hasn't arrived in three days, the American intelligence services will be told what has happened here tonight ... what you've just received. You may think you are safe here on this island. I can assure you, you won't be safe any more."

"You're threatening me," Sarov muttered. There was something at once calm and deadly in the way he spoke.

"It's nothing personal," Carlo said.

Marc produced a cloth bag. He unfolded it, then tipped the money out of the case and into the bag. The case might contain a radio transmitter. It might contain a small bomb. He left it behind.

"Good night, General," Carlo said.

"Good night." Sarov smiled. "I hope you enjoy the flight."

The two men walked away. Marc could feel the money, the bundles pressing through the cloth against the side of his leg. "The man's a fool," he whispered, returning to his own language. "An old man. Why were we afraid?"

"Let's just get out of here," Carlo said. He was thinking about what the general had said: *I hope you enjoy the flight*. Had he been smiling when he said that?

He made the agreed signal, pressing his finger and thumb together. At once the Cessna's engine started up.

General Sarov was still watching them. He hadn't moved, but now his hand reached once again into his jacket pocket. His fingers closed around the radio transmitter waiting there. He had wondered if it would be necessary to kill the two men and their pilot. Personally, he would have preferred not to, even as an insurance policy. But their demands had made it necessary. He should have known they would be greedy. Given the sort of people they were, it was almost inevitable.

Back in the plane, the two men were strapping themselves into their seats while the pilot prepared for take-off. Carlo heard the engine rev up as the plane slowly began to turn. Far away, there was a low rumble of thunder. Now he wished that they had turned the plane round immediately after they had landed. It would have saved some precious seconds and he was eager to be away, back in the air.

I hope you enjoy the flight.

There had been no emotion whatsoever in the

general's voice. He could have meant what he was saying. But Carlo guessed he would have spoken exactly the same way if he had been passing a sentence of death.

Next to him, Marc was already counting the money, running his hands through the piles of notes. He looked back at the ruined buildings, at the waiting jeep. Would Sarov try something? What sort of resources did he have on the island? But as the plane turned in a tight circle, nothing moved. The general stayed where he was. There was nobody else in sight.

The runway lights went out.

"What the...?" The pilot swore viciously.

Marc stopped his counting. Carlo understood at once what was happening. "He's turned the lights off," he said. "He wants to keep us here. Can you take off without them?"

The plane had turned a half-circle so that it was facing the way it had come. The pilot stared out through the cockpit window, straining to see into the night. It was very dark now, but there was an ugly, unnatural light pulsating in the sky. He nodded. "It won't be easy, but..."

The lights came back on again.

There they were, stretching into the distance, an arrow that pointed to freedom and an extra profit of a quarter of a million dollars. The pilot relaxed. "It must have been the storm," he said. "It disrupted the electricity supply."

"Just get us out of here," Carlo muttered. "The sooner we're in the air, the happier I'll be."

The pilot nodded. "Whatever you say." He pressed down on the controls and the Cessna lumbered forward, picking up speed quickly. The runway lights blurred, guiding him forward. Carlo settled back into his seat. Marc was watching out of the window.

And then, seconds before the wheels left the ground, the plane suddenly lurched. The whole world twisted as a giant, invisible hand seized hold of it and wrenched it sideways. The Cessna had been travelling at one hundred and fifty kilometres per hour. It came to a grinding halt in a matter of seconds, the deceleration throwing all three men forward in their seats. If they hadn't been belted in, they would have been hurled out of the front window – or what was left of the shattered glass. At the same time there was a series of ear-shattering crashes as something whipped into the fuselage. One of the wings had dipped down and the propeller was torn off, spinning into the night. Suddenly the plane was still, resting tilted on one side.

For a moment, nobody moved inside the cabin. The plane's engines rattled and stopped. Then Marc pulled himself up in his seat. "What happened?" he screamed. "What happened?" He had bitten his tongue. Blood trickled down his chin. The bag was still open and money had spilled into his lap.

"I don't understand..." The pilot was too dazed to speak.

"You left the runway!" Carlo's face was twisted with shock and anger.

"I didn't!"

"There!" Marc was pointing at something and Carlo followed his quivering finger. The door on the underside of the plane had buckled. Black water was seeping in underneath, forming a pool around their feet.

There was another rumble of thunder, closer this time.

"He did this!" the pilot said.

"What did he do?" Carlo demanded.

"He moved the runway!"

It had been a simple trick. As the plane had turned, Sarov had switched off the lights on the runway using the radio transmitter in his pocket. For a moment, the pilot had been disoriented, lost in the darkness. Then the plane had finished its turn and the lights had come back on. But what he hadn't known, what he wouldn't have been able to see, was that it was a second set of lights that had been activated – and that these ran off at an angle, leaving the safety of the runway and continuing over the surface of the swamp.

"He led us into the mangroves," the pilot said.

Now Carlo understood what had happened to the plane. The moment its wheels touched the water, its fate had been sealed. Without solid ground beneath it, the plane had become bogged down and toppled over. Swamp water was even now pouring in as they slowly sank beneath the surface. The branches of the mangrove trees that had almost torn the plane apart surrounded them, bars of a living prison.

"What are we going to do?" Marc demanded, and suddenly he was sounding like a child. "We're going to drown!"

"We can get out!" Carlo had suffered whiplash injuries in the collision. He moved one arm painfully, unfastening his seat-belt.

"We shouldn't have tried to cheat him!" Marc cried. "You knew what he was. You were told—"

"Shut up!" Carlo had a gun of his own. He pulled it out of the holster underneath his shirt and balanced it on his knee. "We'll get out of here and we'll deal with him. And then somehow we'll find a way off this damn island."

"There's something..." the pilot began.

Something had moved outside.

"What is it?" Marc whispered.

"Shhh!" Carlo half stood up, his body filling the cramped space of the cabin. The plane tilted again, settling further into the swamp. He lost his balance then steadied himself. He reached out, past the pilot, as if he was going to climb out of the broken front window.

Something huge and horrible lunged towards him, blocking out what little light there was in the night sky. Carlo screamed as it threw itself head first into the plane and onto him. There was a glint of white and a dreadful grunting sound. The other men were screaming too.

General Sarov stood watching. It wasn't raining yet but the water was heavy in the air. There was a flash of lightning that seemed to cross the sky almost in slow motion, relishing its journey. In that moment, he saw the Cessna on its side, half-buried in the swamp. There were now half a dozen crocodiles swarming all over it. The largest of them had dived head first into the cockpit. Only its tail was visible, thrashing about as it gorged itself.

He reached down and lifted up the black container. Although it had taken two men to carry it to him, it seemed to weigh nothing in his hands. He placed it in the jeep, then stood back. He allowed himself the rare privilege of a smile and felt it, briefly, on his lips. Tomorrow, when the crocodiles had finished their meal, he would send in his field workers – *the macheteros* – to recover the banknotes. Not that the money was important. He was the owner of one kilogram of weapons grade uranium. As Carlo had said, he now had the power to destroy a small city.

But Sarov had no intention of destroying a city.

His target was the entire world.

**READ OTHER GREAT BOOKS BY
ANTHONY HOROWITZ...**

WELCOME TO THE DARK SIDE OF ANTHONY HOROWITZ

BOOK ONE
He always knew he was different. First there were the dreams. Then the deaths began.

BOOK TWO
It began with Raven's Gate. But it's not over yet. Once again the enemy is stirring.

THE POWER OF FIVE

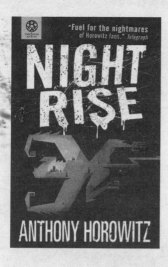

BOOK THREE
Darkness covers the earth.
The Old Ones have returned.
The battle must begin.

BOOK FOUR
An ancient evil is unleashed.
Five have the power to defeat it.
But one of them has been taken.

BOOK FIVE
Five Gatekeepers.
One chance to save mankind.
Chaos beckons. Oblivion awaits.

THE CHILLING POWER OF FIVE SERIES

NEXT IN THE SERIES:

Necropolis

Oblivion

Heading for an exciting new life in London, Tom
Falconer is ambushed by the murderous Ratsey.
Helpless and alone, the orphan gallops towards
the great city, where a number of mortal dangers
await him. But on the first night of a new play –
The Devil and his Boy – Tom discovers that the
fate of Elizabethan England rests in his hands.

"A cracking historical adventure... Thrilling." *TES*

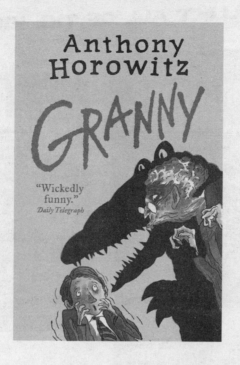

Joe Warden isn't happy. He has rich, uncaring
parents and he's virtually a prisoner in the huge
family mansion, Thattlebee Hall. But his real
problem is his granny. Not only is she physically
repulsive and unbelievably mean, she seems to have
some secret plan – and that plan involves him.

Can Joe thwart Granny's evil scheme before he's
turned into neoplasmic slime?

"Wickedly funny." *Daily Telegraph*

"Hugely popular ... I can hear Horowitz fans
drooling." *The Times*

COLLECT ALL OF THE HILARIOUS

"Horowitz is the perfect writer. His dialogue crackles with hardboiled wit."

Frank Cottrell Boyce, *Guardian*

DIAMOND BROTHERS INVESTIGATIONS

Tim Diamond is the world's worst private detective, and unfortunately for his quick-thinking brother, Nick, the cases keep coming in. What connects them? Murder! And if the Diamond Brothers don't play their cards right, they could be next!

Photograph © Jon Cartwright

Anthony Horowitz is the author of the number one bestselling Alex Rider books and The Power of Five series. He has enjoyed huge success as a writer for both children and adults, most recently with the latest adventure in the Alex Rider series, *Russian Roulette*, and the highly acclaimed Sherlock Holmes novel, *The House of Silk*. His latest novel, *Moriarty*, is also set in the world of Sherlock Holmes and was published in October 2014. Anthony was also chosen by the Ian Fleming estate to write the new James Bond novel which will be published this year. Anthony has won numerous awards, including the Bookseller Association/Nielsen Author of the Year Award, the Children's Book of the Year Award at the British Book Awards, and the Red House Children's Book Award. In 2014 Anthony was awarded an OBE for Services to Literature. He has also created and written many major television series, including *Injustice*, *Collision* and the award-winning *Foyle's War*.

You can find out more about Anthony and his work at:
www.alexrider.com
@AnthonyHorowitz